MERCURY'S CHOICE

Also by Kyler James:
THE SECRET OF THE RED TRUCK

MERCURY'S CHOICE

A Fable of New York City

KYLER JAMES

REBEL SATORI PRESS
New Orleans

A portion of *Mercury's Choice* was published in the journal *Scroll of Thoth* with thanks to Mark Reynolds, editor.

Excerpt from *In Search of the Miraculous* by P.D. Ouspensky. Copyright 1949 by Houghton Mifflin Harcourt Publishing Company. Copyright (c) renewed 1977 by Tatiana Nagro. Reprinted by permission of Houghton Mifflin Harcourt Publishing Company. All rights reserved.

Heartfelt thanks to Sven Davisson, Jessica Wainwright, Janet Reid, Ben LeRoy, Betsy Lerner, Simon Kane, Dennis Cooper, Xavier Villanova, and David Lowenherz.

Cover Illustration: Atelier Sommerland

ISBN: 978-1-60864-131-4

Rebel Satori Press
www.rebelsatoripress.com

Once you have perceived that life is very cruel, the only response is to live with as much humanity, humour and freedom as you can.

— Sarah Kane

SPRING 2001

PART ONE: NEW YORK

ONE

I've always known, ever since I was a little boy, that one day I would kill someone. I never told anyone this, however—not even my mother—or any of my psychiatrists. That's why I'm telling you now from this strange place in which I find myself. Such a very strange place; not at all what I expected. And what a surprise! Life is full of surprises, but death is full of certainty.

Let me begin my story—for I desperately need to tell it—at the Metropolitan Opera, New York City. It was the second intermission of Wagner's *Parsifal*—and I had brought with me a chocolate Toblerone bar to have with coffee outside of the Grand Tier. It was one of the first warm spring nights, the kind of night in New York when you believe that love might really be possible in this world, that the Holy Grail might really be redeemed.

I needed my chocolate and coffee and cigarette to sustain me through the 5½ hours of James Levine's sublime conducting. I inhaled my Marlboro deeply, feeling more alive than usual, filled with the early April night, the soul of Wagner and the grandeur of the Grand Tier balcony, feeling a kinship with the other smokers in this wretched, smokeless city. Being at the Met was always the next-best thing to being in Europe.

And then I saw him: I thought he was German at first; he was conversing with a blond boy in what seemed to be his native tongue; and the only words I understood were "Placido Domingo." I thought they must be together but he shot a look at me—I thought he was offended by my smoking—for he was simply drinking champagne. How could anyone drink at a Wagner intermission? I needed all my energy and wits about me to "endure unto the end."

But this piercing look stabbed my heart and made me semi-hard and I thought: how can I possibly say hello with this blond stud at his elbow? Then I heard the first warning bells and prayed, as if I believed in God, that the boy would run off to the men's room.

But no one at the Met—or anywhere else for that matter—dared to go anywhere alone. It's as if people needed, in armies of twos or threes, protection from a barrage of invaders. Whereas I traveled everywhere around the city alone—totally alone—yet totally free; without fear, yet without companionship.

Yet if God didn't exist, the nearly-full moon seemed to have heard my prayer—and the blond German boy dashed off, presumably to go to the loo. And I was alone—as usual—but this time with the intense stare of this dark, handsome man who was now approaching me. In plain English he asked, "Could you spare another smoke?"

"Sure," I replied and opened the box suavely, for once, as the middle cigarette perfectly popped out in his direction, like a prediction of the excitement to come.

"Thanks," he said, as I lit his cigarette, proud of my successful determination not to tremble as I did.

"What's your name?" I asked, worrying that it was time to go in.

"John," the stranger replied. How boring, I thought, I don't want to meet a John with a blond boyfriend no matter how beautiful a night it might be.

"Do you know a place called Barrage?" he suddenly asked. "Ninth Avenue and 47th Street. It's relatively new. I'll be going there alone after the opera. Would you like to meet up?"

"Sure," I said, as the final bells sounded and we awkwardly pushed our way through the heavy Grand Tier door, rushing back to our seats with the other

True Wagnerites, all those who stayed for the last act of *Parsifal*—but none who would enjoy the slow-moving music with the same anticipation that we would, awaiting our destiny which I somehow knew would be blissful, yet fatal.

OK—I know what you're thinking: that this sounds melodramatic, right? But life *is* melodramatic and this was *my* life—at least the life I knew when I was at the end of my rope. When I needed love so desperately I thought I forgot how to love. When I thought it was something impossible in New York. London, perhaps—Paris, quite possibly. But how can one love in a city where something as natural as smoking is outlawed everywhere? Bizet said, "Life is smoke" in *Carmen*; and so it is—I see that now. *La fumée*: the incense of Mars. Men and lust and strength and power.

I would kill for a cigarette now. But then again, I *did* kill. And yet my desire has gradually faded, faded away like the last notes of *Parsifal*—5½ hours of rapture; 5½ hours of refuge from the world; 5½ hours of pure, idealized perfection; and 15 minutes to my destiny at Barrage.

I arrived at 1 A.M.—just when I liked to have my first Jack Daniels. The place was packed—everyone was smoking: how delightful! Such a good vibe in the place; had everyone just come from *Parsifal*?

Suddenly I saw him: the friggin' liar! He was with the blond boy. No one in this city keeps his word. Our eyes met as soon as I entered; I wanted to turn around immediately but he rose to his feet, knocked into a man lounging in the window and shouted, "Hey, Marlboro Man (I had never introduced myself)—don't go— there was an unanticipated chain of events and Ludwig (Ludwig?) tagged along. Please stay and have a drink with us. We're exhausted."

"All right," I said, knowing how I detested threes: there was always the likelihood of competitive warfare amidst the front of social amiability. How I hated social amiability. One on one, it was possible to be sincere. With three, never. And in a crowd, as Ibsen said, Truth just flies out the window.

Which is just what I wanted to do; but like a coward, I agreed to stay. Don't get me wrong: Ludwig was cute but I did not want to relate to both him and John at the same time.

How did other people do it, I always wondered. They charmingly made the best of their social situations, I supposed. But me, I'd rather go off and drink by myself than laugh with the crowd or camp-it-up with the queens.

Do I sound anti-social to you? Psychopathic perhaps? Well, yes—and proud of it! In a lifestyle that's supposed to be different, there's more conformity in the gay world than you'd ever find in the straight. That's why I prefer straight bars: the men are so masculine and the women so wild. Everyone knows who they are—or thinks they do—and it's all so happy. In gay bars they have to laugh louder than they do in straight bars. They have to screech over the disco music; but I've always preferred the rock-and-roll of straight bars. You see, I'm a True Wagnerite: Led Zeppelin, Nirvana, Radiohead any day over Gloria Gaynor or Madonna.

Anyway, the music wasn't so bad at Barrage and Ludwig was grinning with a very welcoming, if insincere smile—so I sauntered over to the lounge area and asked John to get me a J.D. on the rocks.

So there I was, ready to spend a minute alone with Ludwig, when all of a sudden—who should come bursting through the door—the last person I'd ever expect—would you believe in a million years? My straight former friend Simon from London who invited me to a New Year's party there and never returned my calls to tell me where the party was. What was he doing in New York at a place like Barrage? I tried to turn, hoping he wouldn't see me; I'm not very good at dealing with too many situations at once. But he spotted me with that huge grin of his: "Davis! Davis! What are you doing here, mate?"

"What am I doing here? I live here. What are *you* doing here and why didn't you call me about the New Year's party in London? Oh by the way, this is Ludwig—we just met –and, oh, here is John with my Jack Daniels. John, this is Simon from London, a friend of mine."

I thought I was doing relatively well under the circumstances, handling a mini-crowd of four—since the only place I really wanted to be was back in my $150 seat at the Met.

"Davis, I am *so* sorry I didn't call you on New Year's but my mother arrived again from Amsterdam and I was up to my arse in motherly love."

"Well thanks for letting me know—I understand…I was just stranded in London with nothing to do on New Year's Eve. Thanks a lot. And thanks for the drink, John. Ludwig and I were just getting acquainted. What are you doing in a gay lounge, Simon?"

"Looking for my flat-mate who I'm here with on holiday. He's got all my money and was supposed to be here. Excuse me, gents, while I 'cruise' the pub."

And Simon vanished out of my life once again. Friends have a way of coming and going so quickly; who the hell can you rely on these days?

"John," I said, "I'm feeling ill; if this Jack doesn't give me that Brick click-in-my-head soon, I think I'll have to call it a night."

"Oh, David…"

"Davis."

"Sorry, Davis—don't go: this is so amusing. You're so

adept at handling groups of people."

"Are you being facetious? I hate groups of people. I'm really kind of a loner. Have you read *The Outsider* by Colin Wilson?"

"Yes, I have…years ago; a little too literary for my taste, if you knew what kind of work I do."

"What do you do?" I asked.

"He's an autograph dealer," answered Ludwig with a particularly thick German accent.

"An autograph dealer?" I asked.

"Yes," said John, "I sell letters of famous people throughout history."

"I'm impressed," I replied. "Do you have any of Wagner's?"

"As a matter of fact I do have one that he wrote to Cosima after composing the 'Siegfried Idyll' for her. It's rather touching for Wagner."

"Those letters cost a fortune!" chimed Ludwig.

"I'll bet," I said. "Well, I'd love to see this letter sometime."

"How about tomorrow at three?" John smiled. "Come to my office." And he handed me his card.

This was so unusual for me; I hadn't met anyone in such a long time, hadn't had any relationship in years— and suddenly a bright, attractive, rich guy invited me to his office to see a letter written by Richard Wagner.

You always know when fate has it in for you. It hits you like a bell that chimes, urging you to return to your seat, warning you that the drug of slowly-played music, the narcotic of soothing, calm existence awaits. The bell chimes. You can hear it on the balcony, the smoke-filled balcony under the nearly-full moon, with the space and the air and the interval between the acts: the breathing-space that we all need to survive… until we encounter the next act, the next context, the next chapter….

TWO

The next day I was finishing a painting. I'm a painter, by the way—or rather I was…then. I was retouching the violet nipples—or shall I say, the Ultramarine Violet nipples—of the goddess Diana; I've always prided myself on my breasts and nipples, succulent mementoes of my bisexual days. My paintings of that period were mostly of gods and goddesses rendered in a realist mode, yet with a near-fauvist flavor as far as color was concerned. I loved my work and was starting to receive some recognition. But more about that later.

I looked at the clock: it was 2:20—and being a punctual person, I wanted to be on time for my 3 o'clock date with John. So I kissed Diana goodbye and instructed Mercury, who was flying naked and virile above her, to hold down the fort. I had to dash from the East Village to Madison and 57th Street.

Waiting for the 6 train at Astor Place, there was an all-too-loud female singer with a microphone, singing an old Laura Nyro song I recognized about going to the country and killing her lover man.

How pleasant, I thought, as the train arrived and I began my journey to 59th Street. I took out *The Tragic Muse* by Henry James, a book I was re-reading, for it had had a big influence on my painting years before. A successful politician gives up his seat in Parliament to become a painter. How heroic! Was I any different? I gave up my family fortune, my father's corporation, to do my will in the world. Did I ever regret it? *Non, je ne regrette rien*—and I mean *rien*.

On 57th Street I realized I was getting nervous. I felt like having a cigarette; but since I had worked out strategic times of the day to have my allotted smokes, this was not an option until "tea-time" at 4:30 or so. To me, discipline was everything. As the *I Ching* says, "To become strong, a man's life needs the limitations ordained by duty and voluntarily accepted. The individual attains significance as a free spirit only by surrounding himself with these limitations and by determining for himself what his duty is." And at this moment, my duty was to keep my word about my 3 o'clock appointment with John.

I arrived on the 44th floor at 2:55: I was always early. A friendly woman named Meri answered the door. She informed me that John was delayed in a meeting with a very important client and would I mind perusing the waiting room in the meantime?

"Not at all," I replied and was immediately drawn to a large, glass enclosure on the right-hand wall. Inside there was an impressive-looking letter and two antique pistols. Upon reading the explanation below, I discovered that the display included a letter by Henrik Ibsen, written before the first performance of *Hedda Gabler* in 1890. The letter was an instruction to the actors on the proper usage and deep meaning of the pistols in the play. How fascinating, I thought, but why couldn't Henrik be present himself to explain these things?

At that moment, John entered the room with a famous-looking man whom I recognized from the Academy Awards but whose name escaped me. "Now don't you worry, Mr. Coppola," John said reassuringly, "we'll have the Olivier letter shipped to you right away, just in time for her birthday."

"John, you're the very best," beamed Mr. Coppola, "and thank you, Meri, for being so informative." As he exited, he darted a most peculiar look at me, as if he recognized me from somewhere, but couldn't quite figure out where. A lot of people gave me this look so I was used to it.

"Hello!" John exclaimed, grinning at me, "glad you

could make it, David!"

"Davis."

"Oh, Jesus—Davis, please forgive me; it won't happen again. Meri, please hold all my calls: I'm going to show Mr. Jarvey here some very special letters."

And we entered his private office, which looked like the set of a Noël Coward play: posh sofas, a bar, a mock spiral staircase and elegantly framed photographs and letters all over the walls. "This is gorgeous," I said, as I admired the view of New Jersey. "Who is *that*?" I asked, pointing to a photograph of a bizarre-looking man, dressed like a clown.

"Don't you know?" asked John, massaging my tense shoulder, "That's Salvador Dali at a costume party in Barcelona. You know, Davis, I figured out why you looked so familiar to me: I met you once about two years ago at one of your shows in Soho. I admire your work."

"Well, thank you, John—what a surprise. Let me see, which one was that? Oh, that must have been my show at Caldwell Snyder Gallery. That was my black and white period; you should see what I'm doing now."

"I'd love to," he said, running his hand through my hair, which to me was the most affectionate gesture a person could offer. It seemed to have the effect of massaging all those worry-cells in the brain, making the mishmash inside totally all right.

It looked like he was about to kiss me, which I wasn't quite ready for yet—so I asked, "Where's the letter?"

"Which one? I've got so many! Oh—the Wagner—it's right here." And he escorted me over to an ornate, golden-framed letter hanging on the northern wall with the unmistakable hand of my favorite composer. "Can you read German?" John asked, with a tinge of titillation, knowing that he would soon have the opportunity to demonstrate his prowess as a speaker of many tongues.

Like the night before, he spoke beautifully and then

translated with a touch of mock solemnity: "My darling Cosima, duty calls me once again to the great river of Schumann, my beloved Rhine...."

"Messing around with those Rhine Maidens again, no doubt," I interrupted—and John and I had a good laugh. It wasn't the nature of what I said so much; it was the nature of our being together, the joy we both felt and the absurdity of love in New York.

We laughed together for a long time, smiling at each other, until John suddenly stopped smiling, took my head in his hands, and gave me a strong, masculine kiss. Ah, it was so good! It had been so long since I'd been kissed like that. His taste was deep and clear, like well water; and his scent was clean and sweet, like a summer night in the Berkshires. We started laughing again and then we kissed some more. "How about dinner tonight?" he whispered.

"Oh, I'd love to, but I'm busy."

"What are you doing? May I ask?" he said, tickling my neck.

"Having dinner with my English painter friend. He's painting my portrait."

"Well, can't you change your plans?" John persisted.

"No," I stated with just the right amount of firmness, "I've given him my word."

"How unusual for New York," teased John.

"Well, you've met one unusual dude, man," I said as I playfully punched him in his gut. Nice and firm, I thought. "But I'm free tomorrow."

"You're actually free?"

"No, I'm expensive."

"Oh, I see. Well, I'll have to take you somewhere worth your while. Do you like Raoul's? Let's go there."

"That'd be great, sir. It's a date. What time?"

"How about 8:30?" he asked, opening the door. "Meri, would you call Raoul's please and make an 8:30 for tomorrow? Two in a booth, if possible."

"No problem, John. Matthew Bourne is on line two—do you want to take it?"

"I'd better. Davis, excuse me a moment." And I was back in the waiting room with Meri. She gave me a knowing smile and I wondered how many men before me had John lured into his private office. I thought I'd better say something fast:

"The real pistols used in *Hedda Gabler*, huh?" was about all I could muster up.

"Oh, yes!" replied Meri.

"How much do they go for?"

"The pistols and original letter by Ibsen, framed, are for sale at 75,000. There's a rumor that the pistols are loaded, you know—but John doesn't really believe it. The whole case arrived from Norway just as it is; it hasn't been opened. But we have an alarm on it, just in *case*, no pun intended."

"Fascinating," I replied, "this is some extraordinary office."

The door opened and John rushed in. "Davis, something unexpected has come up. Matthew wants to meet me immediately at The Pierre for tea. He's very interested in the Tchaikovsky 'swan' letter. Meri, please have that ready. Davis, I'll go down with you."

And we descended the 44 flights like a countdown back to reality: New York City, Madison and 57th Street, my new favorite corner of the world. "See you tomorrow, Davis—I've got to run—8:30—Raoul's—be good…."

And he was off without a kiss, handshake or hug. And there I was, ready for "tea-time," ready to celebrate my newfound joy, my newfound love, my newfound exuberance of life! How could I possibly sleep that night? I'd arrive at Raoul's with huge circles under my eyes!

"Calm down, Davis," I said to myself as I purchased an Earl Grey in the deli, "you'll be OK." And on the street

I lit my Marlboro, gleaming and shining like a meteor about to land, smoking with the flames of my long, lonely journey...from outer space down to the real, wonderful world.

THREE

Crash. It was 8 o'clock the next night and I was a total wreck. The circles were indeed under my eyes and I looked terrible, like a cross between Munch's *The Scream* and Picasso's *Gertrude Stein*.

It was the full moon. "Save me, Diana," I intoned eastward over my shoulder, as I walked westward on Prince Street toward Raoul's. I arrived fifteen minutes early so I walked around the block, chanting "Save me, Diana, save me, O Goddess." And at 8:25, I simply had to enter the joint.

What a buzz! The place was humming, the music was sizzling and the smell of the food was…nauseating. I needed some *Côte du Rhone* fast. I went straight to the bar.

There, an attractive English woman asked, "Don't I know you, darling? Tell me, how do I know you, tell me!" She seemed a little over-the-top.

"I, uh, don't know exactly. What is your name?"

"Jessica, darling. What's yours?"

"I'm Davis," I said.

"Hello, Davis—what are you drinking, my dear?"

"I think I'll have a *Côte du Rhone*, thanks."

"Fantastic. Michael, would you give this handsome young man a *Côte du Rhone*, please? He needs it and wants it—I can tell."

"Where exactly are you from, Jessica? I know it's somewhere in England."

"London, darling—but what do you do? How do I know you? Thank you, Michael—here's your *Côte du Rhone*, Davis. Are you an artist of some sort?"

"Well, yes, I am; I've had a few shows around here."

"You have? That's brilliant! I must have seen you at

one. Were you written up?"

"Yes. *The Times* called me the most promising new painter of 2000. Of course I'd been around for years— and that was already a while ago."

"Really! Where can I see your paintings now?"

"Well actually, nowhere at the moment. I'm doing a series of gods and goddesses for my own amusement and I'm not sure where they'll be viewed yet."

"You call me, Davis—let me write down my number… here…I've got a lot of connections and a very strong feeling about you."

"Thank you, Jessica, I'll give you a call—and I mean it. Oh, here's my friend John. Hi, John."

"Hello, loverboy."

"John, this is Jessica from London. Can I get you a drink?"

"Not yet, thanks. Let me talk to the maitre d' and find out about our table. There don't seem to be any at the moment. Excuse me."

"Davis, have you tried the psychic upstairs? She's very good, you know. She's told me many things that have come true. Why don't you try her tonight?"

"Oh, I don't know, Jessica—I don't go in for that sort of thing too often; just a little *I Ching* now and then."

"Well, do yourself a favor and try her after dinner. She's only got one night a week here and she's the living end."

"OK, maybe I 'will do.' Jessica, my friend is beckoning to me—I think we have our table. Thanks so much for the wine and I'll call you…soon."

"So long, darling—have a splendid, romantic dinner. I'll be rooting for you!"

"Thanks, Jessica, you are too much!" And I departed toward the fish tank and our booth.

"Oh, John, it's so good to see you. It's been so long!"

"Even longer for me, buddy. How are you?"

"A little nervous, to tell the truth, but Jessica calmed me down. How did it go with Matthew Bourne?"

"Well, we had a nice tea, but I don't think he was serious about the Tchaikovsky letter; I think he just wanted to go out with me. So I told him discreetly about you...."

"About me? What did you say?"

"Oh, that I just met a talented, good-looking man at the opera and that we were having dinner tonight."

"That's all?"

"What more could I say? I was trying to sell the letter. He's going to consider it, but I doubt that he'll buy it."

And at that moment, Michel, our waiter, arrived to tell us the specials. They all sounded good but we both ordered the steak *au poivre*, which everyone always had at Raoul's.

"Richard Gere is here tonight," said John, "did you see him?"

"No," I said, "I didn't have time to see anyone; Jessica engaged me immediately in conversation. Anyway, I only have eyes for you. They're looking a little tired at the moment; I hardly slept at all last night, I was so excited."

"My sentiments exactly, my man. Ah, here's my wine—what shall we drink to?"

"To destiny...our destiny together...and to Diana, goddess of the full moon."

Then John linked his arm around mine and, looking deeply into my eyes, said: "To our friendship, Davis, may it strengthen us always." And I lifted my *Côte du Rhone*, as he did his *Merlot*, and then we drank to the sound of Moby singing why his heart feels so bad, why his soul feels so bad.

He'll never know, the chorus echoed, he'll never know, he'll never know....

What a great dinner we had; the food was always

15

good at Raoul's. We didn't say that much to each other; we smiled seriously most of the time into each other's eyes. It was that rare, relaxed feeling that you have with someone when there's no need to force conversation.

Over espresso I asked, "Do you think I should see the psychic upstairs? Jessica says she's very good."

"If you like, *mein herr*. Why don't you do that while I get the check?"

"OK, mister—shall I meet you outside then?" And John shook my hand firmly and seriously.

Upon ascending the spiral staircase, it looked like Rozelisa, the psychic, was finishing up with someone. So I gave her a nod, as if to say I'd be next, and ran over to the men's room.

When I returned she greeted me with a radiant smile, which made me trust her instantly, and she gestured for me to sit in the now-empty chair. I paid her up front and she began:

"It's the full moon tonight, in Libra, you know—a very good time for love. Let me finish shuffling…OK… now please cut the deck into three piles," which I did. Then after placing the piles together, she started turning over the cards, about ten of them. I was just fascinated. Suddenly her warm smile vanished and she asked, "Are you seeing someone professionally, sweetheart?"

"Do you mean like a shrink?"

"Um-hmm," she nodded.

"Yes, I am."

"I think it's very important that you continue seeing this person," she said gravely as she slid the cards back together and handed me my money.

"What's the matter?" I insisted, getting quite agitated.

"I'm so sorry, sweetheart, but I strongly think that it's not a good idea to continue. Please be careful and take care of yourself. Again, I'm really sorry."

And my spirits spiraled downward like the staircase

I descended, feeling totally dejected and worried. How could I face John now? But there he was, waiting for me with that handsome smile of his: "What's the matter—you look like you've seen a ghost."

"Perhaps I have: my own," I replied, on the verge of tears. "John, she wouldn't read me—she gave me my money back."

"Oh, come on, chum, don't take that stuff seriously. Let's have a nightcap—what do you say?"

"Would you mind if we didn't do that tonight? I feel like getting back and finishing my painting. Can we see each other soon?"

"I certainly hope so. Are you going to be all right?"

"Yeah, I'll be OK—I just need to paint. I'll call you tomorrow."

"I'll be in the office. And Davis, there's a chance I'll be going to London next weekend. Perhaps you'd care to join me."

"Oh, London—that might just be what I need. We'll see…let's talk."

And we gave each other a really nice hug as I saw him into his cab. There he goes, I sighed, my new man.

The moon had risen high in the sky as I slowly made my way eastward on Houston Street. What could have been so terrible, I wondered, that she wouldn't tell me? Why didn't she just blurt out the whole bloody truth? It would have been better than this stale, depressed feeling that I had in my stomach. But why should I be so surprised, I asked myself; didn't every happy situation turn into its opposite sooner or later? That's why I had to return to the one thing I could always rely on: my work, my art, my fertile oasis…in the blank desert canvas of my life.

FOUR

"My life has been like a blank desert canvas," I told Dr. Myers, as I lay on his luxurious, East 76th Street couch. "So how can I possibly fit my entire week's life into one of these forty-five minute sessions? That's why they call you a shrink—because you have to shrink everything to fit within this time constraint. But I want to *expand*! I want to be like one of the gods I'm painting, doctor. I don't want to shrink anymore. So that's it: this is my last session."

"Why don't we talk about this, Davis?"

"I *am* talking about it. This has been very helpful to me for two years—but I've suddenly realized that it's time to move on, despite the advice of this psychic I saw last night who strongly advised me to stay with you. But why should I stay, being the rebellious spirit that I am, when all you do is say things like, 'Elaborate on that,' or 'What comes to mind now?' Listen: I'll never take medication—so what do I really need you for? Someone to talk to? Well guess what: I'm in love. And I've got somebody new to talk to, who in fact I'll be talking to later. So that's it, doctor, I don't want to pay for this anymore." Then I sat up for the first time in six months and looked him squarely in the face: "I feel great—I'm cured."

"Davis, calm down. You still have quite a few issues that you need to resolve."

"Well, we're in agreement on that, doctor, but you know what? I think I'm ready to resolve them on my own. I don't think I can *grow* here anymore. I don't know where this is coming from exactly, but I feel liberated. I've had an epiphany: I haven't slept in two nights, I've finished one of my best paintings ever, and

I'm in love for the first time in years. What more could I ask of you? You've been very helpful and I thank you for that, really. And now, I'm going to do something outrageous. Instead of begging you for a few extra minutes, I'm going to leave ten minutes early. Don't look at me like that! This is not resistance or avoidance—and don't tell me it's acting out. I'm going to leave early and hopefully never return because, you know what? After this intense depression last night and an all-night full-moon-painting-vigil, the goddess Diana told me I'm finally free. I'm liberated. I am one with my psyche. She appeared to me all in white. She took me by the hand. She led me to her altar of incense and candles and said to me, 'Davis, this is your time now. Go forth.' So thank you, Dr. Myers…I'm going to go now…." And, believe it or not, I got up from the couch and left that office forever. I was a liberated man.

I couldn't wait to call John, but I thought I'd give it some time, sort of cool down a little from my bold exit. I decided to go have a half-pint of Guinness, which I never did in New York in the middle of the day, but always did in London. Why not celebrate? I was on a permanent vacation from Dr. Myers.

The question was: where to go? Telephone, Swift's? There was no gay place in New York that served Guinness, I didn't think. Why not go to Telephone, get my Guinness and call John from one of the big, red telephones? That sounded like a spot-on idea.

So I took the 6 Train from 77th Street down to Astor Place and trotted over to Second Avenue and Telephone Bar and Grill. Who should be there but my English friend James (not the painter) who was also sneaking a mid-day Guinness. All my friends seemed to be English and straight.

"James—aren't you working today?"

"No, Davis, I had a fight with my wife and decided not

to go in."

"Well, you'll never believe this, but I've got a new boyfriend, I think, and I came here to call him like I promised to do, on one of the red telephones."

"Well, congratulations on the new love, but I assure you, it's not what it's cracked up to be."

"I'm sure you're right, but at this stage...I'll believe in anything. May I have a half-pint of Guinness, please—not the cold one."

"Certainly," said the pretty bar lady.

"Do you like her?" I asked James.

"Do I like her? I've slept with her twice."

"How was it?"

"Good—except she's a friend of my wife's."

"Uh-oh," I laughed. "James, this is such a hoot! I'm celebrating three things: I've finished a major painting, I'm in love, and I walked out of my shrink's just now, hopefully never to return."

"Congratulations, Davis. That's how I felt when I walked out of AA—and I've never returned either."

"Let's drink to never returning," I said as my half-Guinness arrived, looking very meager indeed compared to James's big one.

"Cheers," he said, as I realized what a great mood I was in; boy, did I have a tendency to go up and down.

"Well, mate," I said, "I came here to call John—can you believe that's his name—John? But I suppose it can wait."

"No, don't let me stop you. I'm just finishing up and then I'm off to the gym."

"OK, James."

"93, Davis."

"What?"

"93. It's a secret code; I'll explain next time."

"All right, I'll hold you to that, James. 93."

"93." And he was off. And I was ready for my big, red-hot telephone call. I entered one of the booths, inserted my quarter (wishing it were a 20p) and dialed.

"Intelligentsia, this is Meri speaking."

"Hi Meri, this is Davis."

"Hi Davis, how are you?"

"Just great—is John there?"

"No, he's out to lunch at the moment. Does he have your number?"

"Actually not, Meri. Why don't I give it to you? I'll be going home and he can reach me there." So I gave Meri my number and raced home to sit by my phone for what turned out to be 3½ hours.

There's only one way to make the telephone ring, I discovered, and that was to fall asleep. I was having this wonderful dream about the god Mercury. He was flying toward me with his caduceus wand, and he said to me in a beautiful voice, "Davis—you can have my caduceus wand or you can have me—but you can't have both. Choose ye well, now." And just as I was trying to make up my mind, the phone rang.

It was my best friend Angel, the straight, English painter. He had a mock-erudite manner that many mistook for gay. "Hi Angel, you devil-you, you interrupted a really good dream."

"Sorry, Davis, but I called to read you this quotation that I know you'll love. Are you ready?"

"Fire away."

"It's from *In Search of the Miraculous* by Ouspensky: 'In order to help others one must first learn to be an egoist, a conscious egoist. Only a conscious egoist can help people.' Isn't that super?"

"Just a second, Angel, I got a beep. Hello?"

"Hello, loverboy."

"John! Hi! Hold on a sec—I'm on the other line. Angel—gotta go—it's John. That's a fabulous quotation;

21

will you write it down for me?"

"Indeedeth," replied Angel, using one of his favorite expressions.

"Thanks, baby. See you soon." I cleared my throat and took a deep breath. "Hi there."

"Did I catch you at a bad time?"

"No, not at all. How are you, mister?"

"A little crazed; it's been a hectic day—but more importantly, how are you, guy? I've been a little concerned."

"Oh thanks, but I'm fine. I finished my painting last night and today has been terrific. I can't wait to see you. Are you doing anything later?"

"Unfortunately, I promised Ludwig a while ago that I'd take him to the theater tonight."

"Oh, Ludwig."

"Now don't worry, Davis. We're just friends. I know him from Berlin. But listen: I've got some good news. I'm definitely going to London on Thursday. I've got to pick up a Mendelssohn letter that's been waiting for me at Sotheby's. There's a problem with the export license so I have to go myself. Would you like to join me? I've made a reservation for you which we have to book by tomorrow."

"John—this has been the most phenomenal day. Once you take charge of your life, everything seems to happen. I'm just going to say yes. Yes! I'd love to go. Wait: one condition."

"Shoot."

"I'm used to traveling alone, which I enjoy. So I just want to make sure that I'll have some time to go off by myself, to be alone a little, maybe see a friend."

"No problem, buster. I don't want us to be sick of each other by the end of the weekend. Shall I call my travel agent? We're flying business class."

"Whoa. You are some classy man."

"Strictly business, I assure you."

"Oh, I'm sure. I just have one question: how am I ever going to sleep? I'm too excited about everything."

"Just a minute, Davis. Yes, Meri?…Davis, I have a call. How about dinner tomorrow?"

"I won't eat until then."

"Then get some sleep instead. Talk to you tomorrow."

"Bye, John." I hung up the phone and leaped into the air, screaming, "Mercury! Diana! I'm going to London with John! Aaaaaaaaaaaaaaaaah!" I tumbled to the floor and sat there, gazing at my beautiful painting, thanking the gods for my great good fortune.

FIVE

"Supreme good fortune," replied the *I Ching* after asking the book if I should go to London with John: "It furthers one to cross the great water." I had been using the Book of Changes, tossing the three pennies, since my Columbia University days and continually found it illuminating. Its answers were almost always on target.

So it was settled; I was really going. The only problem was—it was Saturday and I didn't have John's home telephone number. With all the excitement, I forgot to ask him for it. I tried calling the office—there was a recording with Meri's voice; and I tried calling information but John had an unlisted number. So I would just have to wait for him to call me.

It was twelve-noon. What should I do? I had finally gotten some sleep and was very excited about our dinner date. Why not give Jessica a try, I thought, and see what she's up to? I refused to waste the whole day waiting for John's call. So I found Jessica's number and dialed it.

"Yes, hello," she answered in a slightly hoarse voice, as if I woke her.

"Hello, Jessica—this is Davis. How are you?"

"Davis, my darling, I'm so glad you called—I was just thinking about you! Did you try the psychic at Raoul's?"

"Uh, yes, I did, but it didn't turn out so well."

"Oh, I'm sorry to hear that, my dear. What happened?"

"Well, let's just say that it was a less-than-thrilling experience. But Jessica, I called to invite you over for tea and to have a look at my recent work."

"Davis, I'd be honored. What day did you have in mind?"

"Are you doing anything this afternoon? I need to be around for an important call."

"As fate would have it, I happen to be free today and would love to come."

"Now Jessica, my place isn't exactly fancy, but it does function as my studio. So no need to dress for the occasion."

"Don't you worry, darling, I've gone to the ends of the earth to see great art, which I expect yours to be—and it's only the art I care about. What time shall I arrive?"

"How's 4 o'clock?"

"Brilliant. What's your address?"

"418 East 9th—that's between 1st and A—apartment 8."

"Lovely. See you at four, darling."

"Looking forward to it, Jessica." And I realized that I had a major cleaning job to do. When was John going to call? Suddenly the phone rang. Oh my God, I must be psychic.

"Hello?"

"Bon-jour," said Angel, in his mock French accent.

"Oh hi, Angel—you always call when I'm expecting John. But that's OK—I love you anyway. How are you, kiddo?"

"Ghastly. Akiko is in one of her moods and started throwing things at me. Can you believe it? (Angel had a thing for Japanese women.) What are you doing this afternoon? May I come seek refuge?"

"Unfortunately, Puss (my nick-name for Angel), I just made other plans. Did I tell you about Jessica from Raoul's?"

"My compatriot?"

"That's right. She's coming to see my work. She's a total delight and says she's got connections."

"Well, I'm furiously jealous. Why don't I show up unexpectedly with a few of my slides?"

"I don't think that would be the greatest idea, much as I'd love to have you—no pun intended. But listen: I've got a major cleaning job to do. Want to help?"

"Cleaning? Are you serious? I'd rather get hit in the head with Akiko's books!"

"All right. But listen, I've got to go. Good luck with the books: maybe some of their knowledge will rub off on you...just kidding. Talk to you later."

And I got out the Comet and the Windex and the vacuum cleaner. Oh, what an entertaining hour I was going to have. What should I listen to? It was a choice between my new *Die Walküre* CD or *Kid A* by Radiohead. I chose Act III of *Walküre*, turned up the volume full-blast, got down on my hands and knees, and scrubbed the bathroom floor to the sound of Birgit Nilsson singing, "Ho-yo-to-ho! Ho-yo-to-ho! Ho-yo-to-ho!" I was truly inspired for an hour-and-a-half of hard labor.

The bell rang at precisely 4 P.M. I still hadn't heard from John and was starting to freak out. "Who is it?"

"It's Jessica, darling."

"Come on up—third floor." And I buzzed her in. After a minute or so she arrived. "Hello, Jessica, I'm so glad you could come today."

"Davis, your timing was impeccable, I can't tell you."

"How so? I thought I might have woken you up."

"Oh no, darling, I had just broken it off with my fiancé and your call did me a world of good. This was the best idea."

"I'm glad, Jessica, but I'm sorry about your fiancé."

"Oh don't be. He was a total wanker like most men—as I'm sure you know."

"I hope I'm not going to be reminded of that today; I'm waiting for John to call me and so far he hasn't."

"Well, I'm sure he will do. Who could resist someone like you?"

"Thanks, you're so sweet. Come have a look…. This is *Cupid Playing with Venus and Mars*."

"Oh, my word!"

"What?"

"It's...I'm stunned. I didn't expect anything quite like this. It's beautiful... and you've got such an eccentric style—your very own."

"Oh, you English are so polite. Be honest with me, now."

"Oh don't worry, Davis, I can be ruthless. What's that one?"

"That's *Pan in the Forest with a Young Satyr,* one of my favorites."

There was a long silence....

"I've never seen anything like it: you really are an original. The color creates movement in a way I've never seen before. I love it: it simply sucks you into the forest!"

"Here's my latest. I'm calling it *Mercury and Diana on the Way to Olympus.*"

"Ohh...Davis, I could faint. May I sit down?"

"Please, let me get you some water."

"No, darling, I'm all right; I'm simply astounded and moved." She took out a mauve handkerchief and began crying. "It's stunning—I just don't know what to say."

"I guess it's been an emotional day for you."

"Do you want to see me get angry, Davis? That's nonsense: it's the painting!" And she began to sob a little. Then she dabbed her eyes. "You are a great talent, Davis. Your work must be seen in a major gallery and I'm going to make sure that it is. Who is that?"

"That's *Apollo: Radiance.*" And I started losing it a bit myself. "This is contagious," I laughed, through my tears.

"Oh, if talent were contagious...we'd have a world of greatness. Instead, we're left with a world of mediocrity. Mediocrity prevails everywhere and in every field. It's up to the few like you, Davis, to fight for your truth and not let yourself succumb to the mob standard. If you don't mind, my dear, I'm not going to stay for tea. Your work has elevated me; I feel more alive because of it. I want to get home right away and make a few calls."

"Oh—are you sure? I've got some nice teas."

"Thank you, darling, but your work has given me a big lift. I'll call you at the beginning of next week. Do I have your number?"

"No, you don't—here's my card. By the way, I think I'm going to London on Thursday for the weekend. So I hope to speak to you before I go."

"Oh you will, darling, you will. And thank you for lifting my spirits." She kissed my cheek and was gone. And there I was, surrounded by my gods and goddesses, exalted and happy, triumphant and serene, with a red telephone by my bed that simply refused to ring.

It was 2 A.M. and John hadn't called. I was at The Cock on Avenue A and I was drunk. Saturday night at The Cock, one of the few places in the East Village I could tolerate. The DJ was great and it was pretty easy—well, *fairly* easy to get laid. They had closed the backroom a while back so I had to cruise around.

There was a dancer on the tiny stage with a rubber jockstrap. Every so often he pulled it down. I watched while I waited in line for the men's room.

"Davis—hi!" said a masculine voice in front of me.

"Jim—that's your name, right?" I said to this muscular, blond stud I'd met once before.

"You've got a good memory, man. You want some blow?"

"I'd love some." So we waited for the private bathroom and did a hit each. Once a year or so I liked to do a little coke; but it was so bad for you, I tried not to do it too often. This, however, was the perfect night. Jim gave me a sexy smile and groped my crotch.

"Hey, man," I said, "I feel a little uncomfortable in here. You want to come over? I live around the corner."

"Sure—that'd be great." And we stepped out onto Avenue A and the waning moon. I couldn't believe that this guy was going home with me. He must be very fucked-up, I thought. But it was just what I needed. Screw being faithful to someone I'd probably never see again. We climbed the three flights and the first thing I did was look at my phone machine; and of course, the light wasn't blinking. Fuck him, I thought, I'll fuck Jim instead!

We tore off all our clothes, did a little more blow, and sat naked, smoking, which was one of my favorite pre-sex turn-ons: smoking was so good on coke! And then—boy, did we go at it! He was a really nice guy, it turned out. It was the kind of sex that was purely fun; we stood up most of the time with big grins on our faces.

And then it was over. "Stay five minutes, will you?" I asked, knowing how so many guys dashed off immediately after sex, as if they had just participated in something they were deeply ashamed of. But I was never ashamed; I took a natural delight in whatever action I chose to do.

"No problem, man," he smiled, as he ran his fingers through my hair, just like John had done a few days before.

I saw him to the door, shook his hand goodnight, and staggered toward my unblinking phone machine to see if someone had called and hung up. I dialed Star 69 but my last caller was Angel. I washed up in my spotlessly clean bathroom, wishing I could wash away the filth of deceit. Do anything you want but don't lie to me, I thought. That's why I couldn't meet anyone: there were no honest guys around in this city. And I, the "great artist," couldn't compromise, had no interest in compromising, would rather be fucking alone than participating in a life of deception.

"So you've got two strikes, John, but who's counting?"

I muttered as I got ready for bed. "I'll go to London with you—if *that's* still happening—but after the third strike, you die. You die, my man, because I'm tired of being lied to. So tired, so tired, so tired...."

And I drifted off into a dark, dreamless daze....

SIX

"Dazed and Confused" was playing on the classic rock station. *Do dare dare dare dare, do dare dare dare dare. Do dare dare dare dare, do dare dare dare: Bom. Bom. Bom.* I played my air guitar as I strutted around my clean apartment. I really ought to keep it this way, I told myself; but then again, I always told myself that after cleaning. Then the dirt would build up for another three months, like a dirty, X-rated desire that needs to be released. *Do dare dare dare dare, do dare dare dare dare.*

I had that edgy feeling I always had the day after doing coke, but felt so good about the time I'd had, it didn't seem to matter. I usually felt good about my sexual escapades (always "safe," of course)—except for the occasional time when I felt I compromised myself in some way. Masculinity was of the utmost importance to me—I liked men, not girls; so if I messed around with someone who was too queeny, I always felt bad the next day. But last night was certainly not a compromise—and as for John, I was practically over him already. I decided he was a total wanker, that my love was just a ridiculous fantasy, and that I would simply move on. I was never really into guys with money anyway; I preferred the starving artist type, somewhat like myself. Too much money seemed to make for a complacency of the soul somehow—and I much preferred men who were searching for something, be it truth or art or even sexual satisfaction.

So feeling like I was practically over John, I decided to give Angel a call. Was it too early? 11 A.M. on a Sunday? I didn't want to invoke the wrath of Akiko and wake her up. I decided to gamble and give Angel a try.

"Hello?" he said in a quiet voice; thank God he answered the phone.

"Bon-jour, Puss, how are you this morning?"

"Glamorous, thank you."

"Angel, would you believe that fucker never called me? But I had some fun in spite of him."

"What kind of fun, Davis, or need I ask?"

"No, you don't need to—the *best* kind. How are things with you and Akiko?"

"Much improved, thanks. We had some fun ourselves last night. The moon was trine Mars, according to my calendar, which was good for sex, if not love."

"Well, that explains everything," I replied semi-sarcastically. "But listen, do you want to go see Blake and Vermeer at the Met today?"

"I was thinking of that myself, but do you really want to be thrust into the masses of a Sunday crowd? All those superficial art lovers with their vulgar comments, shoving you in the side as you try to get a good view of Satan?"

"Good point, Puss, but I'm in the mood to go anyway. What do you think? We could always leave and work on my portrait if it gets too obnoxious."

"That's true. I just hope Akiko will understand. What time shall we meet up?"

"How about 2:30 on the front steps?"

"That sounds like the quintessence of perfection. 2:30, then."

"Until then, mate." And I was so glad to be seeing Angel on a Sunday, which I was rarely able to do. I loved Angel like the brother I never had. When I met him in London, the day before he was moving to New York, I thought he was gay; but upon meeting him in New York—and discovering that he was straight—our friendship blossomed in a platonic way and kept on growing ever since.

I showered and dressed for our Sunday outing with very little thought, if you can believe it, about John and whether or not he would call. I locked the door behind me, descended the first flight and thought I heard my telephone ring. "That's got to be my imagination," I told myself, as I kept on going down the stairs. "I refuse to sacrifice my dignity by running up there and making a fool of myself. Even if it is John, I'll get the message later. I refuse to think about him for the whole afternoon. I devote this day to art, to friendship, and the finer aspects of life."

And with that resolve, I landed on a very sunny East 9th Street and decided to get a Stromboli's pizza slice, my favorite, on St. Marks and First. While having my slice outside, who should be walking by but my friend James with a man and woman dressed in black. "James—93! Where are you off to?"

"Oh hi, Davis, 93. This is Pat and Sam."

(Pat seemed to be the guy, while Sam was the girl.)

"93, David," Pat and Sam both said.

"It's Davis with an S—James, what does 93 mean? You were going to explain it."

"Well, we're in a bit of a rush," he said. "We're off to a Gnostic Mass. Do you want to join us?"

"I can't today; I'm going to see the Blake and Vermeer shows at the Met."

"Oh, William Blake is one of the saints in the Gnostic Mass," Pat said.

"What is all this?" I asked. "What is a Gnostic Mass?"

"James, why don't you explain this to Davis when we're not running so late?" Sam suggested. "Davis, we're sorry, but we're really running behind and we have to set up for the mass. Once a month there's a public one, so perhaps you'd like to come next month."

"I think I really would, Sam. So James, let's talk. 93, you guys, have a good one."

"93, Davis," said James.

"93, Davis," said Pat.

"Nice meeting you, Davis, 93!" said Sam.

And they were off and I was very amused. I couldn't wait to go to this Gnostic Mass and find out what 93 meant. But for now it was the 6 train again. That singer with the microphone was there, only this time she was singing Led Zeppelin's "Dazed and Confused." Life is just too weird, I thought, as the train arrived and I began my journey uptown, wondering what further surprises this Sunday would have in store for me.

Now if I told you that I met John on the front steps of the Met as I was waiting for Angel, you wouldn't believe me and would say it was much too contrived. So I'm not going to tell you that I met John on the steps—because I didn't; but I did think about the possibility, even though I promised myself not to think about him for the entire afternoon. I'm pretty good with my promises in general, but not thinking about someone is a very difficult promise to fulfill. Anyway, Angel appeared quickly enough so I was able to forget about John once again.

We thought we'd tackle Blake first, since Angel didn't like his drawing that much; but the crowd was so horrendous, you could hardly get a complete view of any work. We agreed that the Satanic watercolors were the best—poor Satan! He was so jealous of Adam and Eve! My favorite was *Satan, Sin and Death: Satan Comes to the Gates of Hell*; but I also liked *The Angel of the Revelation*, which they used to advertise the show.

We made our way to the second floor with the throngs of Sunday art lovers. It was good to know, at least, that so many people appreciated art. Someday they'll be flocking to see *my* work, I thought.

The Vermeer show was even more crowded than the Blake, if you can imagine that, and it was getting to be a little much for me. We spent some time sitting on the bench in front of *Christ in the House of Mary and Martha*, the truly great painting of the day. The look in Christ's eyes, whether you believed in him or not, was enough to break your heart. So visceral, you could almost hear the deep sound of his voice and feel the warm touch of his pointed finger. Now there was a man. Strong and sensitive, masculine and tender, with the power to heal in his eyes. Sitting there with Angel and this painting was the highlight of my day.

Two typical-artist-types walked right in front of us and stared at the painting. "It almost looks unfinished," said one of them to the other, "as if the painter had anticipated the gestural qualities that began perhaps with Goya, reached its pinnacle with Picasso and disappeared entirely with contemporary art's obsession with flat color."

Angel rolled his eyes. "Rudeness and idiocy seem to go hand in hand," he whispered.

"The worst part," I added, "is that they're completely missing the experience, trying to sound intelligent to each other."

"They couldn't sound intelligent if they tried," he laughed.

Every group of people, it seemed, had its own particular jargon: painters, actors, therapists, new-agers. It was as if no one had the courage to express his own views in his own words. It was common to every one of society's social clubs, no matter how intelligent or erudite they might appear to be. That's why I tried whenever possible to express myself in my work and my speech with my own voice.

We decided to call it a day and go have some tea in Central Park. The beauty of the warm, spring afternoon and the afterglow of experiencing Great Art were upon us. We strolled silently, like the characters in *La Grande Jatte*; and although there was a quarter in my pocket and a telephone by the boathouse, I had absolutely no desire to check my phone machine; in fact I wanted to avoid contact with it for as long as possible. Freedom from one's phone machine was equivalent to freedom from one's life—at least on Sunday.

But the inevitable was upon us, and soon it was time to part ways: Angel to the east and I to the south. I took the Fifth Avenue bus, the slowest way I could return home, and tried to prepare myself for the harsh reality of a tiny, green light. My entire life's fate, it seemed, rested on the importance of what this little light was doing: to blink or not to blink—that was the question. And in 45 minutes I would discover the answer.

The light was blinking. Oh, my God. Ever so calmly, I removed my shoes, removed my shirt, my pants, my underwear, and slipped into my comfortable boxer shorts. Ever so calmly, I approached my phone machine and pressed Play. I could tell that a very long message was rewinding:

"Hi Davis, this is John. It's 1 P.M. on Sunday and I'm calling from my office. I am so sorry and feel just awful about what happened, but I forgot to take your number home with me; I had left it here on my desk. We both have non-published numbers, and neither of us had them, obviously. Yesterday my cat got very sick and it was a grueling scene at the vet's and I was not able to retrieve your number until today. I feel so bad about this and want to make it up to you. I hope that you're OK; I've actually been a little distraught and I look forward to hearing from you. I booked our tickets to London and I hope that you still want to go with me. You are a very fine man, Davis. Please call me when you get this; I should be home by late afternoon, early evening. Here's my number…."

Well, well, well. Did I smile? Did I cry? Did I just stand there aghast? I really don't remember. Those moments now seem like a warp in time. Did I feel like a fool? Was I overjoyed? I played the message again: he sounded very sincere. I played the message a third time: he sounded like he was making up a good story. No he didn't; he sounded like he was really in love with me. Or was this just my projection?

I've never been a vindictive person; and like Nietzsche, I've always despised vindictiveness in other people; but I was simply not able to call John that night. I had been so hurt, I realized, thinking I was being rejected—that I simply was not able to turn my emotions around so fast.

As I look at it now, from this quiet, contemplative place, I wish I had called him. It might have made all the difference. But we see with larger eyes from a distance than we do with our everyday, narrow vision. Had I been able to paint myself in those lost moments, my self-portrait would have been as Parsifal, the Pure Fool, with a dying swan in the background—and the Grail being offered to me for the very last time.

PART TWO:
LONDON

SEVEN

The last time I'd flown business class was years before, returning from Paris with my former patroness, Elizabeth, a wealthy woman in her seventies. We didn't know it at the time, but she'd had a heart attack in Paris—her doctor informed her of this back in New York—and I was able to convince the flight attendants to upgrade us, since she was feeling so ill. (She liked to spend her money on the arts, not the airlines.) When I set my mind to it, I could convince anyone of almost anything.

But it didn't take much convincing to realize that John and I were the "class couple" of business class, holding hands listening to Mendelssohn's *Italian Symphony* on the headphones as our British Airways jet took off for London. It didn't matter that it was one of the most overplayed symphonies in the repertoire; when the lilting *Allegro vivace* perfectly synchronized with our swirling past Manhattan and our veering eastward toward Long Island, our hearts soared with the music and the rising plane—and we knew we were in for a wonderful trip together. After all, it was thanks to Mendelssohn that we were going in the first place.

John's hand felt so warm and strong around mine, an acknowledgement of our first heartfelt talk together about that anxious Saturday when we couldn't reach each other. We'd both been so honest about our insecurities that it brought us to a place of true intimacy, seeming to set us on the right track of trust for the future. (I didn't tell him about my Saturday night, though, nor did he tell me about his Sunday night, I'd discover much later.) His cat, Lima Bean, had recovered from its kidney infection and was being watched over by a caring neighbor.

Jessica had called on Tuesday in a whirlwind of excitement, informing me that two dealers from Gagosian Gallery would *probably*—she stressed the word probably—be paying me a visit after my return to view my paintings! She didn't want to promise anything but it was looking very hopeful. So all being well in the world of cats and canvasses, we settled into our very comfortable seats, so cozy and happy that I didn't even think about my first cigarette at Heathrow.

We both ordered the lobster—how wonderful it was to dine in business class!—accompanied by two delicious white wines and finally, a sauterne for dessert. I was ready for dreamland. We snuggled up as best we could without being too outrageous, and the last music I remembered hearing was the slow movement of Beethoven's 7th Symphony....

To the tune of this somber *Allegretto*, John and I walked hand in hand on West 24th Street toward Gagosian Gallery. As we entered the gallery a fanfare of trumpets sounded with red banners waving everywhere. All my paintings were there, only they were giant-sized. There was Angel, Jessica, my parents, my high school art teacher—everyone was there to greet us. Photographers from *The New York Times* were there to take our pictures for the society page.

Suddenly the 3rd movement started and Mercury flew out of his painting and appeared before me: "Davis, oh Davis—I have brought you splendid, speedy success! Now choose: my caduceus or me! What will it be, Davis? What will it be?"

"Mercury, my god, may I have a moment to confer with my boyfriend?"

"If you must, mortal artist that you are, but make it snappy."

"Thank you, Mercury. John, would you possibly understand if I chose to be with a god? After all, he *is* a god."

"That's fine, Davis, as long as *you* understand that I'll be with my *own* god." And suddenly Ludwig appeared out of the shadows, smiling his insincere smile.

The music changed once again. Mercury flew very close to me and offered his caduceus wand, which turned into a gun the moment I touched it. Everyone in the crowd gasped. Suddenly they were all waltzing around us to the tune of the Beethoven *Presto*. We whirled around and around, making a huge funnel, a tornado on West 24th Street. The tornado traveled westward into the Hudson River, carrying all of us into it. We spewed upwards, like the waterspout of a whale, and suddenly I was alone with Ludwig, the gun pointing directly at his head.

The triumphant 4th movement started. Mercury flew back to me, grabbed the gun, which immediately turned into the caduceus—and we were all back in the gallery as Mercury reentered the painting. Champagne corks were popping everywhere! Streamers were streaming! Flashbulbs were flashing! John and I were triumphant! Angel and Akiko were ecstatic! Jessica and her fiancé were reunited! Life was beautiful, great and true! Life was magnificent! John and I swirled and swirled, kissed and kissed—and we entered the painting, traveling with Mercury and Diana to Olympus. We were just about to meet Lord Jupiter…when I suddenly woke up to John saying:

"Davis, Davis, hey, hey, are you OK, my man?"

"What—John, oh, I was having a fantastic dream—you were in it."

"Well you were humming Beethoven very loudly in your sleep! Sorry to disturb you, buddy."

"Oh, no problem, mister, you can disturb me anytime." And I put my head on John's shoulder and proceeded to have the soundest sleep I'd ever had flying, thanks to my man beside me on the night flight to London.

I was used to taking the Underground from Heathrow to Earl's Court, where I usually stayed; but this time a taxi brought us directly to The Park Lane Hotel on Piccadilly near Hyde Park Corner. What a thrilling way to enter the city in the early morning! We had taken one of my favorite scenic routes along Kensington Gardens and I always gaped like a real tourist at the Albert Memorial, which I loved. More often than not, I brought good weather with me, so we both wore our sunglasses.

John tipped the driver who said, "Cheers, mate," and we entered the hotel which was not quite as attractive as I'd imagined; but I was so high that nothing in the world seemed to matter: London was definitely my drug of choice.

We entered our spacious room overlooking Green Park—and I was titillated with joy beyond belief. Neither of us thought of sleeping; John wanted to go to Sotheby's first thing and get that out of the way—and I didn't care what we did. London was to me the most vital city in the world: all the arts seemed to be happening and thriving in a way that put even New York to shame. We had theater tickets, museums to visit—and for once I had absolutely no desire to go off by myself, even though it was the condition I'd made to John the week before.

We washed up, brushed our teeth, hugged each other tightly—and I whirled us around, pushing John onto our large bed and kissing him real hard on the neck. We still hadn't made love, which was something very exciting to anticipate. John laughed and starting slapping me around:

"Come on Davis. Let's hit the road. We've got plenty of time to fool around later."

"OK, Big Bad John," I said, "let's be off!"

It was such a gorgeous day, we decided to walk along

Piccadilly all the way to Old Bond Street where Sotheby's was. I was usually pretty happy in London, but this time I could hardly contain myself. I had never been to Old Bond Street before; all the fancy stores like Cartier were there. Under normal circumstances they held no interest for me; shopping was my least favorite activity. But being with my special man put a different perspective on these events and I wouldn't have minded actually buying a shirt with him, if it had come to that.

We entered Sotheby's and John seemed to know right where to go. We turned into an alcove that had a pick-up desk with various parcels behind it. "Hello," John said to a smartly dressed woman behind the counter, "I'm John Cunningham from Intelligentsia in New York and I'm here to pick up a Mendelssohn letter, lot #689 from your sale on March 23rd."

"Mr. Cunningham, we've been expecting you. I see the item has been paid for; may I see some form of identification, please?"

It was wonderful to observe John handling the situation, so handsome and self-assured, such a pleasure to behold. And to think that this man might be in love with me! Like Jessica, I could have fainted on the spot. John signed for the letter after inspecting it; it was written in English, to my surprise, during one of Mendelssohn's visits to London. The woman wrapped it carefully and then we were off to The Tate Britain to see the Stanley Spencer show.

We walked to the Green Park tube station, right next to The Ritz, and took the Victoria Line south to Pimlico. It was only two stops. I always loved it when they said in such proper English, "This station is Green Park. Change here for the Piccadilly Line." You had to hear *me* do it: I had it down perfectly. And John had plenty of opportunities since I announced it along with them at practically every station.

As many times as I'd been to The Tate, I always got a touch lost, having to turn so many corners from the Pimlico tube station. We passed a nice-looking pub on the way, the White Swan, and I said to John, "Oooo—let's go there for our first Guinness after Stanley Spencer." I had this notion that the iron in Guinness was good for jet lag—and whether it was true or not, I preferred to believe it.

Elizabeth had taken me a few years before to see the play *Stanley* on Broadway. I had found it so tedious that I left at intermission, which made Elizabeth furious. But I liked his work; a little on the intellectual side, I thought, but quite psychologically probing. His self-portraits were especially honest; and when we were ready to leave, I went back and reviewed the five individual ones, beginning with age 23, and was quite taken with the progression. John was left a little cold by the show, but read me Spencer's last words printed in the program: "Sorrow and sadness is not for me."

"Me neither, Stanley," I replied, "me neither."

We made our way to the White Swan to have half-Guinnesses and our second cigarettes of the day. I loved to sit in the pubs and watch the cute English boys (or were they Australian boys?) in action, serving the drinks and food so politely. They were the very best in the world, I thought; but being there with John, I watched them a little less. It was so good to sit there with him, smoking and smiling, quite a different experience from my usual "werewolf of London" state of mind.

We decided that we'd better not overdo it on our first day, so we agreed to go back and unpack, maybe frolic in the park a little before High Tea at five. My friend Stephen, a set designer, had gotten us tickets to *Hedda Gabler* for that night, having worked with the design team at the National Theater before it transferred to the West End. It was supposed to be the "snob hit" of the season—and we hoped that we wouldn't conk out in the middle of it.

Naps were forbidden on the first day; they really seemed to throw you off, as I'd experienced the one time I tried it. So after unpacking, we took a short bus ride over to Kensington Gardens—we wanted to take advantage of the nice afternoon and I wanted to show John The Serpentine Gallery. The sculpture of Chen Zhen, the Chinese conceptual artist, was being exhibited. I liked it; John didn't. I was beginning to suspect that we had very different taste in art. But we were having such a good time together that taste didn't seem to matter.

We strolled through Kensington Gardens, all in bloom, and passed by the Peter Pan Statue, which John had never seen. I was starting to feel a little woozy, so we decided to head back to shower and dress for tea and theater.

How do modest American men react upon seeing each other naked for the first time? I tried to be nonchalant about it, but was betrayed a little by my rising caduceus wand. John laughed and slapped me with his towel. "Nice one," he said, as he started his shower in our luxurious bathroom, while I picked out my attire for the evening. Choosing clothes was not my forté; I really couldn't be bothered. So I picked out my black jeans and nice shirt and was done with it. It was my turn to shower and it smelled so good in there with all those scented accessories they give you.

When I emerged, John was nicely dressed, as always, so I threw on my clothes and we were off to The Lanesborough Hotel on Hyde Park Corner, my favorite place to have tea in London. I had gone there once with Elizabeth and some friends. The huge conservatory was exquisite, its décor inspired by the Brighton Pavilion. They were out of crumpets but I didn't care; there were plenty of sandwiches, scones and desserts—and we both got a nice tea buzz, which we hoped would last us for the evening. And of course, it was so pleasant to be able to smoke wherever we sat.

What was the nature of our conversation together? I can't exactly say that we discoursed on grand intellectual themes, the way Angel and I did; but there was an intelligent perkiness to our talks combined with the ardor of our growing passion for each other that made for a splendid liaison between us.

It was time to venture on to Theaterland. *Hedda Gabler* was playing at the Comedy so it was an easy ride on the Piccadilly Line to Leicester Square. I couldn't wait to say, "This station is Leicester Square. Change here for the Northern Line," which I promptly announced as we reached our destination.

The theater was a short walk from the tube station. I'd seen such good productions of Ibsen in London, like Alan Bates in *The Master Builder*, so I was excited to be seeing Francesca Annis as Hedda. Stephen had gotten us excellent seats—fifth row center stalls—so if we didn't nod off, I was sure we were in for a great treat.

The performance was outstanding, the best *Hedda* I'd ever seen, but I swore I'd never see a show on my first night again because no matter how wide awake you thought you were, as soon as the lights dimmed, the temptation to fall out was nearly inescapable. So John and I did doze a bit, being ready to poke one another if we sensed that a snore was forthcoming.

For years I remembered that my favorite line in the play was: "Do it beautifully, Eilert Løvborg, with vine leaves in your hair." Ever since my high school History of the Drama class, that line stuck in my head, referring to Hedda's encouraging Løvborg to kill himself "beautifully" with her pistol. So I was waiting to hear the line. Perhaps it was the translation but it appeared that my memory was totally false: the line was completely different. Funny how memory can play tricks on you.

"Don't tell Stephen," I whispered to John, "but *your* pistols look so much more authentic."

"That's because they *are* authentic," John whispered back.

There was nothing quite as satisfying as good theater in London; you couldn't even compare it to New York. I always felt that my life was improved because of it; that the greatness of the artists, on stage and off, permeated my mind and spirit, encouraging me to do the very best in my own art. Experiencing excellence was always an inspiration for achieving it.

John had ordered a bottle of expensive champagne on ice, which was waiting as a surprise in our hotel room when we returned. What a lovely way to finish such a phenomenal, if long day. We popped the cork and drank to the ecstasy of London. We stripped off our clothes, pulled back the covers—and with no thought of making love, got into bed like two army buddies, drunk with the victory of a glorious battle—and fell asleep with our arms entwined, dreaming that we were special lovers, destined to be together for a long, long time.

EIGHT

We spent a long, long time at The British Museum the following morning—too long, if you ask me; but John wanted to see the Cleopatra of Egypt show, which was terrific, and then we couldn't seem to leave. We stumbled upon the crystal ball of John Dee, astrologer to Queen Elizabeth I, which was my favorite surprise of the morning. (Soon to follow was my favorite surprise of the afternoon.) Next to it was his "magic mirror," which he supposedly used to invoke the angels. "Do you see anything in there?" I asked John.

"Yes, I do."

"What do you see, sire?"

"I see a half-pint of Guinness across the street at the Museum Tavern."

"I don't see that. But I can taste it. Let's go!"

So we took a quick walk through the Great Court and crossed the street to the Museum Tavern. I had been there a few times and, as always, the young man behind the bar was even cuter than the time before. While we were having our Guinness and smoke, this strange-looking fellow with very distinct features entered the pub and walked towards us to ask the cute bartender a question:

"Excuse me, mate, I've been looking for the Atlantis Bookshop, somewhere on Museum Street. Would you happen to know it?"

"It's just down there," pointed the barman, "on the left-hand side."

"I appreciate that. Cheers, mate. 93."

"WHAT!?" I exclaimed, as the strange fellow dashed off. "Excuse me," I said to the bartender, "Do you know what 93 stands for?"

"Haven't got a clue, mate, sorry."

"John," I said, "Let's drink up. We've got to get to the Atlantis Bookshop right away! I'll explain later."

The façade of the Atlantis Bookshop was a beautiful, deep blue with words like "magic" and "occult" printed over the window. As we entered, I immediately noticed a huge statue of an animal god, the Egyptian Anubis, we discovered later. The smell of frankincense filled the air; hypnotic chant music played in the background; and there were books everywhere arranged in different sections. The bloke who had entered the pub seemed very busy in the "Rune" section, so I immediately walked over to the bald man sitting behind the desk and said, "Excuse me. I keep hearing the number 93 being used. Do you know what this means?"

"I do know what it means," said the man with a twinkle in his eye, "but are you sure you're ready to hear the answer?"

"I think so," I said, looking at John who had a disbelieving smirk on his face.

"It could change your life," warned the bald man. "Are you sure you want to know?"

"I think I can handle it; what do you think, John?"

"I think we're ready for anything. Why don't you tell us?"

"All right, then. It's the numerological equivalent of the Aleister Crowley phrase, 'Do what thou wilt shall be the whole of the Law.' If you add up the letters in a certain way, you'll see that they come to 93."

"But what does it mean?" I asked.

"It means that there is only one commandment and that is to discover and do your will in life, your highest and truest will. All great men throughout history have done it; yet it's a total negation of the Judeo-Christian ethic."

"Wow. How do you say it exactly?"

51

"Do what thou wilt shall be the whole of the Law, with a capital L. It has a corollary phrase, a response, which is 'Love is the law, love under will.' It would do you well to contemplate these ideas."

"Is it Satanic?"

"Not at all. It's actually quite a noble law, very Nietzschian—and very few people know how to live up to it. We've got a number of books in the Crowley section, if you're interested."

"Thank you very much," I said. "What do you think, John?"

"I think we should go back and consult the crystal ball," he replied sarcastically.

"I don't know…it sounds pretty intriguing to me," I said as I walked toward the Crowley section. I picked up *The Law is for All* and browsed through it. "Angel would like this, I bet—I think I'll get it for him."

So I purchased the book and we were off to Old Compton Street to have crêpes for lunch. It was drizzling but I thought we'd be able to sit outside under the canopy. The sun came out by the time we arrived—you could never predict the weather in London—so we sat under the canopy anyway.

"Which crêpe shall I have, Davis?" asked John. "They all sound so good."

"Do what thou wilt shall be the whole of the Law," I replied. "I'm going to have the spinach and cheese."

"Well I'll have the same: love is the law, love under will." And John gave me a big kiss on the mouth right out on Old Compton Street.

Our crêpes were energizing but we decided to take a short nap before our big night of theater. We had tickets for what was arguably the hottest (and coolest) night in town: Sarah Kane's last two plays, *Crave* and *4.48 Psychosis* at the Royal Court in Chelsea. I had met Sarah once before she died at the opening of my show at Caldwell Snyder Gallery. I'll never forget what she said to me; it was one of the sweetest comments I've ever received. In the midst of my opening, where no one was really paying attention to the work, where it was all about the social scene, Sarah came right up to me and said, "Even though your paintings are black and white, it's so apparent that you feel the color of life so deeply, so deeply that you have to conceal it; it would be too painful otherwise. But your paintings are really full of color." I'll never forget that and I wish I could have known her better.

We actually managed to nap for about half an hour but John kept tickling me; and giggles didn't seem to mix very well with sleep. So we gave up on that and ordered some tea instead. We still hadn't made love but I had the feeling "tonight's the night." We did our tea and smoke and shower routine and soon it was time to head over to Sloane Square. Our taxi dropped us right in front of the Royal Court Theater, where Sarah's name was spelled out in red neon lights.

My last show at the Royal Court had been David Hare's *My Zinc Bed* and I'd had some amazing pumpkin soup downstairs in their restaurant; so I suggested that we grab a bite there before the two plays. It was good to be dining with the people you knew you'd be sharing a theatrical experience with, mostly a young, hip crowd in this case as opposed to the more stately West End audience at *Hedda Gabler*.

We both ordered the lamb curry—we seemed to always want the same dishes—and I took that as a good sign, so different from my past dining-alone-with-fish-and-chips trips. We shared an apple tart for dessert, along with espresso and smokes; and soon they announced that *Crave* was about to begin. I got all excited—there seemed to be much more of a buzz in the theater than the night before—and we walked up one flight of stairs to our comfortable, red leather seats in row J of the stalls.

Crave was really captivating; the four actors had the level of excellence I'd come to expect in London. But nothing would have prepared us for the final lines of the play. I was used to having uncanny coincidences in London; something about the vacation high seemed to create them. But we totally freaked out when the main male character suddenly said: "Do what thou wilt shall be the whole of the Law." John and I turned towards each other and then quickly turned back upon hearing, "Love is the law, love under will." We grabbed each other, as if we were seeing a horror film, and the play ended soon after that, leaving us speechless.

We had a half-hour before *4.48* started; you couldn't really call it an interval, for you needed separate tickets for the two plays. And it's a good thing we had them because *4.48*, unlike *Crave,* was completely sold-out. It was Sarah's last play, written right before her suicide, and it seemed like all of London wanted to understand her better. In an odd sort of way, John and I felt we were a bit closer to this understanding, for on some level we knew that Sarah truly did her will.

We climbed a flight of stairs, purchased two coffees from the bar, and took them outside on the balcony overlooking Sloane Square. What did we just experience? "Brilliant counterpoint," John said, "infinite longing."

"Color disguised as black and white," I said. And we looked at each other as only two people could who were still alive and didn't understand what death and suicide were about—and I knew we thought the same thing at the same time, that we substituted our fear of the incomprehensible with our feeling we'd found the answer: that we were in love with each other.

In those moments on the balcony, we kissed like we'd never kissed before—and we didn't care at all who might be watching. "Thank you for this trip, John," I said, our coffee getting cold.

"You're welcome, Davis, I'm glad you could come with me."

And they announced that *4.48 Psychosis* was about to begin.

There was nothing to be said afterwards; I'd never seen anything like it before and I cried like I'd never cried at a play before. What could you say about a beautiful, hour-long poem about depression and suicide? John and I left the theater holding hands, knowing that we'd witnessed something that was new and important in drama. We had planned on going to Brompton's in Earl's Court; so as if we were hypnotized, in total silence, we made our way downstairs to the District Line and took the train three stops west.

When we got to Brompton's neither of us felt like going in, so I suggested that we walk a bit by the cemetery across the road, which was reassuringly calm, even if it was closed at that hour. We held hands as we walked outside the gates and we both cried a little. Why did this world have to kill off its sweetest and most talented people?

Like Sarah in the play (and presumably in real life), we refused to medicate ourselves—at least not right away; we preferred to stay sober for a while with the intense feelings that were stirred up. But when we entered Brompton's it was time to succumb and I ordered a double Jack Daniels on the rocks. So did John. It was incredible to be in Brompton's with an actual boyfriend; there was no need to hunt around. I loved the gay scene in London: it all seemed so happy and carefree—even the music was more playful than New York. I'd often considered moving there but realized it was just the illusion of what I called vacation mode, that the thrill would probably wear off after a few months.

It was difficult to fully join in the spirit of the club and I was glad John was there to share the same sentiment. We decided to take a walk in Earl's Court before heading back to our hotel; it was strange not to be staying around the corner at The Philbeach, the gay hotel where I usually stayed. We taxied back to The Park Lane and I couldn't believe that our short weekend was almost over.

Back in our room, I poured us some Jack Daniels, and we knew it was time to be together. We slowly unbuttoned and unzipped our clothes. We kissed with the desire to empower each other, to make each other stronger, like men of ancient Greece or Rome. Our lovemaking was more like wrestling: two men naked and hard, wrestling. What a turn-on! I'd always been happy with mine—but his was tremendous, just like I'd imagined.

We shot off into the air, screaming with the joy of triumph: we both were victorious! Isn't that what we live for really? Those moments of passion when we're so alive that we're not alive; so ecstatic for a few moments that we actually transcend the pain of living?

With a large Park Lane towel, John cleaned away the juice of life from our bodies; and we fell asleep on our king-sized bed, dead to the world of Saturday night revelers, all blessed by Eros at Piccadilly Circus, all longing to be loved.

NINE

Longing to be loved in the morning was the same as longing to be loved at night; the desire never seemed to fade away. And there was something about having a strong arm around you as you woke up on a London morning that seemed to make everything in the world safe, secure, so nice. That's why most people craved relationships, I mused as I lay there; they didn't have the canvas and paints to sing their souls to sleep at night.

Though there was nothing better than John's strong arm around me, even if it interrupted my sleep, while he slept on and on. Wasn't it always that way? They all seemed to sleep so soundly, those men of the past— while I stayed awake to experience every nuance of a man, it being such a rare occasion that one would actually spend the night.

He squeezed me tighter, and even though it kept me awake, the soothing quality was worth more than all the sleep in the world: nothing could be more reassuring than the feeling of being loved in the morning, although it was, sadly, our last morning of the trip. That night I'd be sleeping alone in my bed on East 9th Street—and all the gods and goddesses couldn't compete with this real life god of mine.

I reached down to feel if he was as hard as I was…and, ooo! Could it be that he'd actually grown overnight? I didn't want to wake him; but then again, I didn't think he'd mind if I went down on him—I simply couldn't resist, safe as I always was—so I went ahead and heard him moaning softly: he had to be awake by now.

Suddenly he sprang up, pinned me down by my shoulders and went down on me in return. Usually I hated morning sex: bad breath, looking terrible, having to pee; but with John, heaven was heaven—so it was best to take Janis's advice and "get it while you can."

There was a lot more tenderness than the night before; I felt like he really cared for me this time. And when we came together, as we did the first time, he cried, "Davis, Davis, my man...ahhhh!"

What a thrill he was on that trip, as I look back on it now. How idyllic the beginnings of a relationship can be. And how they can sour so easily, like milk left out for a cat to lap up in the middle of the night. Knowing this to be true, even then, I was determined to lap up all I could, because something inside told me it was too good to last.

This time it was my turn to get the towel; I used the same one as the night before, hanging on the back of the bathroom door as Sarah had hung, a newspaper article said. I brought the towel to our bed and we cuddled together in a warm afterglow, fading back into sleep for another half hour until it was time to face reality: the last day of our London trip.

The good thing to be said about every last day in London was that they were always, without exception, sunny. Based on this knowledge, I used to plan little outdoor excursions to places like Hampstead Heath, knowing that I could always leave my umbrella in my packed suitcase at the hotel. On this Sunday, though, John and I decided to visit The Saatchi Gallery, where the controversial Liane Lang video was showing. I loved controversy and the fact that Scotland Yard's Obscene Publications Unit had nearly shut down the gallery made it even more enticing.

We took the Jubilee Line north to Swiss Cottage and it was a nice walk to The Saatchi. I had phoned Stephen to thank him for the *Hedda* tickets and hoped he understood that my relationship with John was just too new to invite him along. I never liked mixing old friends with new lovers. We arrived at the gallery—I had been there once before to see the "Neurotic Realism" show—and it was swarming with ultra-cool London types, somewhat similar to the audience at the Royal Court. I always loved to go where the cool crowd went; it helped *me* to feel cool, which I never really was at all.

We found Lang's video, called *Masturbation*, amusing; but we couldn't sit through all sixty minutes of it. Perhaps if we'd been heterosexual we might have drooled for more, the masturbation being of the female variety. It was simply an animated hand and vagina made out of what looked like bright pink Silly Putty with black plastic pubic hair. There were plenty of titters in the audience as we moved on to Grayson Perry's pornographic pots. As always in London, watching the people—and hearing them talk—was every bit as good as watching the art.

We decided to have our last half-Guinness at the Victoria pub on Abbey Road and I persuaded John to walk down to the touristy spot in St. John's Wood where the Beatles crossed the street on their *Abbey Road* album. If you faced north, it looked exactly like the famous photograph, except for some of the cars. We avoided buying the T-shirts, but couldn't resist traversing the crosswalk with long strides of our legs, just as the fabulous four had done, while we sang "All You Need is Love."

Sadly, it was time to retrieve our bags at The Park Lane and catch our taxi to Heathrow. We passed Hyde Park Corner with its grand arches, The Lanesborough Hotel with its fiery torches, and Kensington Gardens with its Albert Memorial, golden and shining in the sun. I would always remember London this way for I would never return there again. And I tried to suppress my feelings of sadness, it being my shortest trip ever: short, but oh, so sweet.

Back in business class, John and I toasted with a fine *Saint Émilion*. For some reason, I always liked to have white wine going and red returning; better for the jet lag, I theorized. And after a wild weekend, red was good to knock you out. We had some great chicken korma to go with it and tiramisu for dessert. Then we settled back in our seats with some *Remy Martin* and put our headphones on, getting all comfy-cozy with each other.

They were playing *Also sprach Zarathustra* by Strauss. Was the music better in business class or was it just British Airways? After the well-known *2001: A Space Odyssey* introduction, I started to fade away....

We were in the palace of Queen Elizabeth I. John Dee was there with his crystal ball, wearing a beautiful headdress and looking just like the man from the Atlantis Bookshop. He was bowing to the queen, whom I realized was a previous incarnation of Sarah Kane. Suddenly the entire court turned to John and me, both of us dressed in modern attire. Dr. Dee slowly approached us with his crystal ball and I started to get very nervous.

"Do what thou wilt shall be the whole of the Law!" proclaimed the astrologer.

I couldn't seem to find my voice so John answered, "Love is the law, love under will," which seemed to put everyone at ease.

"Who is the man known as Davis?" asked John Dee.

"It is I," I managed to say.

"I have a special message for you, Davis. But first, what is the password?"

"93, sire," I stated, with a little more confidence.

He turned toward the queen who looked impressed as she handed him his magic mirror. "What do you see in this magic mirror, Davis?"

"Uh...nothing, I'm afraid, sire."

"*What* did you say?" he asked angrily—and there were

murmurs in the crowd.

"Stop all this nonsense!" ordered the queen as she approached us. "Davis has not been properly trained for the mirror, John; show him the crystal instead."

"Very well, your majesty," Dr. Dee humbly replied. He held up the crystal ball, which started glowing with a powerful white light. All the torches in the palace dimmed as the white light grew stronger and stronger. The music swelled and a gong sounded and Mercury appeared looking dashingly handsome, naked of course. He flew before us with his caduceus wand, while everyone watched in awe.

"I am Mercury, god of magic! Who is the one that has dared to paint my image on a canvas?"

There was silence in the court as John gave me a little shove. "It is I, Lord Mercury. I am the artist who has honored thee."

"In the name of Queen Elizabeth, John Dee and William Shakespeare: I thank you for the honor, Davis. But now the time has come to choose. The gods have blessed you with divine talent and this is not something we take lightly. Therefore, choose: my caduceus or me! Choose now, Davis!"

"Choose now, Davis!" commanded the queen.

"You'd better choose," whispered John.

"But I don't know what to choose!" I cried, as my tears started flowing for all to see. "I don't know what to choose!"

"Very well, Davis," replied Mercury. "You will be severely tested in the next months. Your life will be put to the test. We will see if you pass it. We will see if you are strong enough. We will see if you are great enough. It will be the most difficult time of your life. Will you pass or will you fail? Will you choose or will you perish? I leave these questions to you, Davis. Hail and farewell!"

"Hail and farewell!" echoed the court as Mercury

61

disappeared in an explosion of orange flames.

As the torches resumed their fire, John Dee said very sweetly, "You had better listen to Mercury; he is a very important god. Now come dine with us, gentlemen. We are delighted to have you as our honored guests."

So the queen, the astrologer, the autograph dealer and the painter ascended the golden stairway that led to the Magical Chamber of Art, where only the truly privileged were allowed. And the last thing I remember was Queen Elizabeth turning to me and saying, "The use and choice of color is crucial, Davis. It is what distinguishes the individual from all others. Do you choose to be a king, a god? If so, my dear, you will have to pay the price, the price of royalty."

And we entered the Magical Chamber of Art as the music died away and the lights faded to black....

PART THREE:
NEW YORK AND BEYOND

TEN

Black were the days to follow after returning home; not black and white—just black. Mercury had been right: I was entering the darkest period of my life, despite the excellent news from Gagosian Gallery. Two dealers did indeed come with Jessica to view my work—and as unbelievable as this may sound, they wanted part of my God and Goddess Series for their group show late June. There had been a cancellation, leaving just enough room for my four large canvases, the ones Jessica had seen. You'd think I'd be happy, wouldn't you? Well, I was for one day—but just wait. Good news always comes in surprise packages.

It was a Saturday afternoon at the end of April, the day after my wonderful news from Gagosian Gallery. Angel was over finishing my portrait, which I hadn't yet seen. I had been posing for nearly four months, sitting practically naked on my throne-like chair, assuming the air of a Roman emperor. The moment for unveiling had arrived and both of us were filled with the anticipation that only fellow artist/brothers could have. I had felt such love for Angel during those four months; his painting me was his way of making love to me—and the closest the two of us would ever get to that.

"Are you ready, Davis?" Angel asked, his blue eyes glistening like beautiful twin stars.

"As ready as I'll ever be, Puss," I replied, my heart beating quickly.

And I rose from my throne, walked to the other side of the painting, took one long look at it…and absolutely hated it. "Angel," I said, "I look so sinister…I've got a double chin…I'm positively scowling."

And thus began the saddest period of my life: the collapse of our friendship. I don't know how I could have handled it differently. In the weeks to follow he tried to fix the painting; but we could never agree on what needed to be done. Angel always thought it was finished and I always thought it needed work. He tried his best to please me but finally walked out one day after an argument over my left eye. I tried calling him but he hung up on me after I accused him of being "fucking stubborn." Like the feud between Van Gogh and Gauguin, ours was impossible to heal. So I sent him this letter as a last resort:

Dear Angel:

I'm feeling such sadness and despair over our situation that I thought I'd try to write you. Every artist—or just about every artist in this day and age—needs two things in his earlier years: continued training and study with a teacher that he trusts—and some form of therapy or analysis for at least two years. I have been in the unfortunate position, as your model and also your best friend, of having to be your teacher to some degree, having been trained very strictly—and also having been analyzed to the point where I think I know myself pretty well. You do not choose to continue your study, nor do you choose to seek therapy. You do not choose to see or read any of the works I recommend on the artist and his plight. This puts me in a difficult and frustrating position.

It's my love for you that makes it even more difficult. Your hanging up hurts me a lot. I know you want to stick to your will about the painting; and I've simply got to respect that. But this letter is not really about the painting. Our friendship has reached an impasse because I feel that in my 10 years over you, there's just too much I've painfully learned that I'm unable to impart. But as Glinda in The Wizard of Oz *says, "You wouldn't have believed me; you* had to learn it for yourself."

There's no question that you've got talent. But you know my philosophy is how to turn the talent into "genius"— how to turn the A- into an A or the A into an A+. That comes from unceasing and relentless work. The artist is never satisfied: it can always be better. Genius is not something you're born with; it's something you work for. I know it seems that you've been pushed and pushed to please my vanity; but that's just one interpretation. I've pushed and pushed because of my love for you—and my love for the painting that we are creating together.

The work never ends. With my own work, I can't sleep until every dab of color is perfect. My former psychiatrist said this wasn't neurotic, but healthy. I may love a painting of mine, but if there's one tiny problem with it, that'll be the only thing I'll notice until it's fixed. It's the same with your painting: I've come to love it, but can't help noticing that left eye, which to me is totally out of focus. I've decided to keep the painting regardless of what you choose to do with it—and it is your choice—but wouldn't it be better if any flaws were corrected before it's framed? To me, pride and ego are positive qualities—but not false-pride or "stubborn" ego. The painting has kept getting better every time we've "forged ahead." Don't you want your art in general to be the very, very best it can be—always?

These are issues to think about. You may decide one day that you don't choose to be a painter. Whatever you choose is OK, but do know that the nature of the artist is to never be satisfied. The nature of the artist is to pull out one's hair, to tear down the ceiling as it were, until that thing called art can be expressed: perfectly, beautifully, with complete vision—and only when it's perfect can you sleep at night; for then the gods can bless you and tell you that everything's all right.

Love, Davis

His response, much later, was simply this:

Dear Davis,

I have had much time to contemplate recent events and feel I can only concur that we have indeed come to an impasse. I wonder at how you would view your own actions of late if they were the actions of another.

The decision has not been an easy one to come to but I feel I must ask for the return of my painting. It is, despite all, a painting I am proud of, and as the artist, can only consider it rightfully mine in accordance with the laws of logic, nature, morality, and will.

Please leave the painting outside your door when you awake on Saturday; I will collect it from there that afternoon.

Angel

It's hard to say which hurt more: the losing of my best friend or the souring of my relationship with John, for they both occurred simultaneously. From the very start, John seemed to take Angel's side.

We were having dinner at Pastis on the Saturday in June when Angel walked out. Attempting to have an intelligent conversation over the noise, John insisted that I try to be more sensitive to Angel's point of view. Looking back on it now, I can see the value of his opinion; but at the time I wanted to encourage the very best in Angel and saw any sympathetic approach as weakness.

Our conversation began to turn into one of our first arguments: "You're so full of yourself, Davis—you're so self-involved."

"Well, you know, you've made your fortune off the souls of self-involved people. That's one of the things that made them great in the first place, that made their letters worth something years later."

"It doesn't suit you to talk nonsense, Davis."

"It's not nonsense, John. What kind of person do you think becomes a genius? Mr. Nice Guy allowing his best friend to settle for less? How bourgeois!"

"You really can be arrogant, you know that?"

"Yes, I do. But what do you suppose got me to the point where I could have four paintings showing at Gogosian Gallery? By being nice and sympathetic—or by being passionately self-involved, as you call it, staying up all night and bleeding over my canvases? Which quality will make my letter to Angel worth thousands one day?"

"I can't talk to you when you're like this." And he got up to go to the men's room. But I knew who won the argument, miserable as I was.

John paid the check, as usual, and we exited onto 9ᵗʰ Avenue. We had spent every weekend together since London, sometimes at my studio and sometimes at his duplex on Park Avenue. We had become quite an item, but on this unhappy Saturday night, the first of many, I wasn't sure what I wanted to do.

I finally broke our silence with: "Well, there's plenty to do in this neighborhood. We could go to The Lure, except you're not dressed for it—or we could go to J's, except it's too early—or we could go to the straight sex club across the street…."

"Davis, maybe we should just go our separate ways tonight."

"You know, John, I was hoping for some support after this day with Angel. But I realize that you've taken the point of view most people would take. If you read the text of *Crave* that was in our program, you might remember the line, 'I hate the consoled and the consoler.' That line was also borrowed from Crowley, I discovered, when I read the book I got for Angel. I refuse to be the consoler, trying to encourage weakness when I want to encourage strength. I know this makes me seem like the bad guy, but I really want to encourage Angel's greatness."

"Maybe Angel doesn't want greatness. Did that ever occur to you?"

I was silent; he had finally gotten to me.

After a few moments I said, "Let's just call it a night tonight, OK?"

"Do what thou wilt, Davis."

"Love is the law, John." And I waved goodnight as I walked eastward on 13th Street.

I walked eastward on 13th Street until it ran into a small park at Greenwich Avenue. I walked eastward on Greenwich Avenue until it ran into 8th Street. I walked eastward on 8th Street until it ran into St. Marks Place. I walked eastward on St. Marks Place until it hit First Avenue. I turned left onto First Avenue and took the first right onto my block. I unlocked the black-iron door of my building, my citadel of power against the rest of the world. There I would stay, as my dark time of loneliness began, ready to produce the works that I would leave behind.

ELEVEN

Behind me stood Felix, the barber, at the Atlas Barber School on East 10th Street. At Atlas, I'd been getting some of the best haircuts I'd had in years for only four dollars; but the first time Felix cut my hair, I hated it and had a fight with him. Soon after, though, I found this cake with green letters saying, "Happy Birthday, Felix"—and brought it to him as a peace offering. He'd been giving me great cuts ever since.

So on this Monday afternoon after my first dismal weekend away from John—and the beginning of my estrangement from Angel—I told Felix to chop it all off. As Kurt Cobain said, he was so lonely, but that's okay, he shaved his head.

With each new clipper that Felix used, I started feeling just a little less depressed. As I looked in the mirror at the rest of the barbershop, I began having the strangest sensation. Was I beginning to lose it? There were three bald men—or nearly bald men—in a row, each having his haircut by a different barber. The mirrors, three men and three barbers made a fascinating juxtaposition, as if one could see through to another dimension beyond the mirrors. And why were three bald men—or nearly bald men—getting their haircuts? The spaces between the mirrors and the reflections upon the reflections hypnotized me to the point where I thought I might be going insane. But I realized I was envisioning my "artist's way of seeing," and that there was only one solution: I had to paint it immediately. As soon as I got home, I decided, I would begin.

I gave Felix a big tip and raced home to stretch a large canvas. The title of the painting was already in my mind: *Atlas Barber School.* I liked the allusion to Atlas holding up the world, this absurd world we live in, where barbers learn to cut the hair of bald men, the mirrors refracting images of blurred reality. This painting would begin my "Absurdity of Life" series; and more than my upcoming show, it was the only thing that kept me sane—if you could call it sane.

Little did I know at the time that *Atlas Barber School* would be hanging in The Whitney one year later, right near the Edward Hoppers on the fifth floor. But I'm getting ahead of myself, aren't I? Sometimes it's so tempting to give things away; I like to drop little hints occasionally. I turned on the radio as I got the canvas ready. Miracle of miracles: they were playing "Lithium," my favorite Nirvana song. To me, Kurt was King. And I became entranced in my sketch of *Atlas Barber School*, my head nearly as bald as the three in my future masterpiece.

At 10 P.M. the phone rang. Who could it possibly be? I had just finished my sketch, was ready to start the actual painting, and didn't want to talk to anyone. I decided to screen the call:

"Hi. This is Davis. I'm either painting, having sex, or taking drugs. Please leave a message after the tone. Thanks."

"Hello, Davis, this is Ludwig. (Ludwig? How did he get my number, as if I didn't know?) I hope I'm not disturbing you, but I thought I should tell you that John's cat died today and he is very upset. (Don't laugh; this isn't funny.) Please call him when you get this message. I know he would like to hear from you. Thank you. Bye."

Oh, fuck. Now I would have to call John, just when I was ready to begin painting. Should I wait until tomorrow and pretend I didn't get the message? No, that would be too cruel; I had to call him. So I dialed his number.

"Hello?" John answered.

"Hi John, it's Davis."

"Hi Davis, I'm glad you called."

"Ludwig told me about Lima Bean. I'm really sorry. How did it happen?"

"It was his kidneys again. Davis, could you possibly come over tonight?"

"Oh, John. This is a difficult time. I'm...in the middle of something important. Can we see each other tomorrow?"

"Well, yeah, I guess that will have to do."

"Would you like me to come to your office at the end of the day?"

"No, you don't have to; why don't I call you around seven when I get home?"

"That's fine. Are you OK?"

"Not really, but I'm hanging in there. It's just so sad; it's worse than losing a friend."

"I know what you mean, John. I miss you."

"I miss you too, buddy. So I'll call you tomorrow then."

"OK, my man, I'll be thinking of you."

"Bye, Davis, thanks for calling."

"Bye, John."

And I got out my Jack Daniels and Marlboros, ready for a long night of intense work.

It was 5 A.M. and it was starting to get light outside. I looked at my canvas and hated what was there. I felt like throwing it out the window—and jumping out after it. I decided that the whole idea was ridiculous. A stupid, fucking barber school: I must be really crazy! I poured myself another Jack Daniels and lit another cigarette. I was starting to drink a little too much, I thought, and it was beginning to concern me. I wished I could die: why didn't I just go uptown and see John tonight? We both would have been so much happier. But no, I had to stay here with my work, my work that would have been brilliant had Ludwig not interrupted me.

Oh Davis, I thought, ease up on yourself, come on, let's get ready for bed; I've got all day tomorrow to start the painting from scratch. From scratch? What a wasted night! What a pathetic excuse for staying up late! And how could I possibly stop working by seven, even if I succeed in rescuing this amateurish fiasco of art? Come on, Davis, ease up, let's go to bed, it'll be better tomorrow.

So I got into bed and lay there, miserable, wishing I could die, wishing I could be somewhere other than New York, the East Village, America. And I started to cry, missing John, missing Angel, missing Lima Bean, missing my work most of all, missing the feeling of being loved; and knowing somehow that it would never be the same with John again. I faded into an oblivion of dark mirrors blending into each other.

Mirrors blended and faded and blended and faded. Suddenly—in between the mirrors—there was something terrifying: Mercury appeared looking very stern. I gasped and woke up, the sun shining brightly on my face.

Tuesday morning had dawned—and with it the bright truth of necessity: I would restart my painting if it was the last thing I did; and above all, I would love it, love it more than anything, more than life itself—and I realized then what Mercury's choice meant: and I was ready to make it very soon.

TWELVE

Soon after falling back asleep, the phone rang. It was 9 A.M. Who could be calling me so fucking early? I let the machine take it: "Hi. This is Davis. I'm either painting, having sex or taking drugs. (Oh shit, that message was supposed to be just for the weekend—I forgot to change it.) Please leave a message after the tone. Thanks."

"Hello Davis, it's Jessica. I hope I'm not disturbing you. Please call me as soon as possible. *The New York Times* wants to photograph one of the four paintings today and give you a brief interview for the Sunday preview article. I'll be at my flat for most of the morning; otherwise, try me on my cell. Bye, darling."

Oh no! Now I'd never get started on the painting today—and that was the only thing in my life that mattered. How could I possibly put it off another day? I couldn't say no to *The New York Times* and I couldn't say no to John again. And what could I possibly say in an interview that was honest? To please get out of my house so I could continue my work? Oh, fuck, fuck, fuck: let me make some coffee.

On the way to the stove, I caught sight of my monstrosity of a painting. "And you call yourself an artist, Davis?" I said. "You ought to go back to Painting 101." Boy, I needed my coffee, but refused to light a cigarette until it was ready: those were the rules.

I sat down with my coffee and smoke, cleared my throat and phoned Jessica.

"Yes, hello?"

"Hi Jessica, it's Davis."

"Hello, Davis, how are you?"

"I've seen better days, my dear, how are you?"

"I can't complain; I've met someone. But I'll tell you

about him another time. What time is good for you today?"

"No time—just kidding; how's three?"

"Fantastic. I'll be arriving with Chris, the photographer, and Julia, the journalist. They're both lovely. Pick out which painting you'd like photographed. I think the *Mercury and Diana*—what do you think, darling?"

"Yeah, I guess so; whatever you think."

"Davis, you sound awful. Is everything all right?"

"Not really, but I'll pull it together by three. And Jessica, I'd like to take you out to dinner for all of this."

"Oh, not necessary, darling, but I would enjoy that sometime. Let me run and call *The Times*. See you later."

"Bye, Jessica."

I put out my cigarette, gulped down my coffee and went straight to my tube of Zinc White. I squeezed out an enormous blob of it onto my palate; and with the largest brush I could find, obliterated version #1 of *Atlas Barber School*, never to be seen again by the eyes of anyone, alive or dead.

By 3 P.M. I had showered, shaved, cleaned a little—and was simply in the most sociable of moods. By the window stood *Atlas Barber School*, completely Zinc White. Maybe I should just leave it that way, I thought, like the controversial painting in the play *Art*—and then I wouldn't have to do any more work on it. I could keep the title and everyone would marvel at the metaphor I created, a barber school of pure, white light. No chance in hell, Davis.

The buzzer rang and they were on their way up. Thrills beyond thrills. Let's be charming, Davis. You don't have an article in *The New York Times* every day.

As usual, Jessica cheered me up right away. "Hello, darling. This is Chris, the magical picture man, and Julia the wiz journalist, both here to spend a little time with our future star."

"Hi Chris, I'm Davis. (He was really young and cute.) Hi Julia. (She seemed like a total sweetheart.) Welcome to my studio. Would anyone like some tea?"

"No thanks," they all seemed to say at once.

"Let's take a look at those paintings we've been hearing so much about!" grinned Julia.

"OK, folks, here they are. Jessica and I both think you might like this one for the photo: it's called *Mercury and Diana on the Way to Olympus*. What do you think?"

"Davis, it's wonderful!" exclaimed Julia. "Which one do you think, Chris?"

"Well, I love them all, but I think my favorite is this one. What's it called, Davis?"

"*Apollo: Radiance.* It's really up to you, Chris."

"Tell you what: why don't I shoot both of them—and maybe they'll print both. The colors will look so nice on the front of the Sunday 'Arts and Leisure' section. Yours are by far the most colorful works of the show."

So Chris began snapping away while Julia began our mini-interview. Jessica seemed radiant: was it her new man or the thrill of having set all this in motion? "What would you say is the most important gift you could give to the art world, Davis?" Julia asked.

"What a difficult question, Julia!" I laughed. "The most important gift I could give? Well, my work, of course, which includes my heart, my mind (both conscious and subconscious)—and my soul. In other words, all of me: I give myself."

"That's a beautiful answer, Davis. And an unselfish one. What are your notions of the artist as being a selfish individual?"

"I'm so glad you asked that, Julia. It seems to most of the world that the artist *is* selfish, totally self-absorbed. But this very quality of selfishness is necessary for him to do the greatest giving of all: to give his (or her) gifts to the world, which include the deepest stratum of his being, his very essence. To me, this is the greatest giving, and ultimately—paradoxically—the greatest unselfishness."

"Thank you, Davis," beamed Julia, "that's all I need. It's been really nice meeting you; your work is splendid."

"Thank you, you guys, are you sure I can't offer you anything?"

"No thanks, Davis," said Chris, "we've got deadlines. Deadlines!"

"Tell me about it," I confessed. "I've got self-imposed deadlines; they're even worse!"

"Let's talk soon, darling," Jessica said as she hugged me goodbye.

"Without a doubt," I whispered. "I want to hear about you-know-who. Bye, folks, thanks for coming!" And they were gone. Whew! I think I got through it OK. And with a boost of my mood to boot! "Now what to do," I said as I marched toward my white canvas. "What to do, indeed. What to do?"

I began mixing colors on my palate; and like a normal, sane, unselfish person, decided to work for three hours until I heard from John.

The phone rang at seven; he certainly was reliable. But the painting was exceedingly difficult; I had set myself a nearly impossible task. I didn't want to stop but answered the phone anyway. "Hello?"

"Hi."

"Hi John. How are you today?"

"About the same; a little better. Would you like to come over for dinner? I'm making *linguini al pesto*."

"Oh, I love that. Shall I bring some wine?"

"If you like."

"John, I should tell you now: it'll be good to see you, but I can't spend the night. I've started a new painting and it's really hard."

"*What's* really hard?"

"The painting, sir. Ha, ha. See you about eight?"

"See you then."

"Bye."

So I washed up, dashed off to Astor Wines and Spirits, and took the 6 Train uptown to my boyfriend's house.

Now I'm sure you'd like a description of John's fashionable duplex apartment, and our candlelit dinner with *Parsifal* playing in the background, and our hot and heavy love session after ice cream and espresso; but frankly, the memory of that evening is just exhausting to me. I was there for one reason only: to comfort John in his state of mourning. And the one thing that was gnawing at my mind the entire time was getting back to my studio as soon as possible. People just don't understand that when there's work to be done—it needs to be done!

So finally I was back with *Atlas*, trying to recreate the experience of hypnotized insanity that the scene produced. The trick of it all was with the mirrors and spaces between the mirrors. I swear, it was the most difficult challenge I'd ever encountered. I contemplated including myself in it, the way Stanley Spencer did, but decided to keep it simpler and leave myself out of it.

After about two hours of solid work, I was ever-so-slightly beginning to be pleased. I was pretty tired and preferred to do my painting with a "full" libido, knowing that I always put my sex drive into my work. As Kurt says in that song, he's so horny, but that's okay, his will is good. How did he know to write stuff like that? Another suicide full of wisdom. And since I wasn't horny, my will wasn't that good; so at 2:30 I decided to leave the party while I was still having a good time and get ready for bed. A little sleep could only help my work the next day.

I poured a J.D. and lit a smoke, reviewing my new

painting. Not bad for a start, I thought. And I got into bed, much less depressed than when the day began, with the bright light shining on my face.

Salvador Dali, I had read, got his inspiration from the hypnagogic state of sleep, that hallucinogenic time between sleep and wakefulness. And as I drifted off once again, I became fascinated with the interplay of mirrors, the Alice Through the Looking Glass of the subconscious. Where did it go, I wondered; where did it lead us? To the insanity of the mind? To the insanity of the barber school? To the insanity of the world held up by Atlas? Only Mercury seemed to know the answer: he was far less stern this night. He seemed to be offering himself in a grand gesture of conciliation, his wand outstretched and within reach, his body open and inviting. He smiled at me with a friendly look of benevolence, as if to say, "It's OK Davis, you're getting closer to it, you're getting to where you need to be. And I'll be here for you when the hour arrives, when the ending arrives, when you find yourself at peace, at last, with your consciousness, the mirror within your mind that you call your self…."

THIRTEEN

"You call yourself a genius?" John asked rhetorically over the phone.

"I never said that," I answered, "a loner, maybe; I would never call myself a genius."

"Well, you intimated as much. And does that make you too good to come to my dinner party? The first one I've had since I've known you?"

"John, since you've known me, I haven't been in the middle of a major painting. The night of our first date I was finishing one, and then you seemed to understand my need to go off and do it. But now your point of view is a little devoid of profound understanding."

"I really don't think it's asking too much; a couple of hours..."

"Just a second; I have another call. Hello? Hello?" No one was there. "John?"

"Yes?"

"Nobody was there. What were you saying so eloquently?"

"The sarcasm is not necessary, Davis. I would like my boyfriend to be there, that's all."

"Well, I'm sorry, John; or to be really honest, I'm not sorry. I've got to work on my painting this weekend— all weekend. I simply couldn't take a dinner party; I couldn't possibly be social. You haven't known me when I've been working—I haven't done any real work since we've been dating—but this is the real me."

"Oh, the real you; I see."

"Do you? You're not interested in the actual process an artist goes through—only that he's worth something."

"That is completely unfair."

"I left my work the other night because I knew you

needed me; but I can't do it again, not at the stage I'm at. Please try to understand."

"I understand that you're a selfish, spoiled son-of-a-bitch." And he hung up on me. Well, well, well. At least maybe I could have some peace and quiet now. It was Thursday and I'd be damned if I were going to a dinner party on Saturday night, boyfriend or not. I planned to lock myself up for the whole weekend and work on my barbershop until I got it right. If John couldn't understand, then fuck him. The telephone rang; it had to be John, calling to apologize.

"Hello? Hello? Who is it?"

Again there was nobody there.

The painting was really coming along, I must say. I was particularly pleased with the reflections of the reflections. Of course there still was an infinite amount of work to be done, but I could see the hypnotic effect beginning to take place. There was a transcendent, luminescent quality that filled me with the only happiness I was capable of having at the time.

Uh, oh: the phone rang. Better let the machine get it, I thought.

"Hi. This is Davis. I'm either painting or sleeping. Please leave a message after the tone. Thanks."

"Hey, it's James. 93. Are you there? Well, I just wanted to tell you about the Gnostic..."

"Hi, James, 93. (I had told him all about the Atlantis Bookshop.) What's happening?"

"Not much, Davis. How's it going?"

"Pretty awful, except for my painting. Were you calling to tell me about the Gnostic Mass?"

"Oh yeah. There's a public one this Sunday, if you're interested."

"I might be, depending on what shape my painting is in. How long is it?"

"About an hour. Would you like the address?"

"Sure; let me write it down."

"It's at Musical Theater Works, 440 Lafayette Street, 4th floor at 2 P.M."

"Well, I just might make it; I'm desperate for something new and exciting. Do I have to know anything in advance?"

"Not really; you already know the most important thing and that's the meaning of 93. The mass will encourage you to do your will in a big way."

"Great. I could use some encouragement right now."

"There you go. Oh—the one thing I should tell you: everyone present has to partake of the sacrament, a cake of light and cup of wine or grape juice. It's important to the integrity of the ritual that everyone participates."

"I have no trouble with that. James, this sounds more and more intriguing."

"The cakes are really good, too. I think you'll like it. I've been in some of the worst moods and have come out feeling elated. You'll see."

"Yeah, I think I'll probably be there. Thanks for letting me know. I should get back to work, though."

"Do your will, Davis."

"93, James. See you on Sunday…probably."

"93."

Well: something to look forward to in my dark, solitary existence. By Sunday, I was sure I could spare an hour.

The phone rang again; without thinking, I answered it.

"Hello? Hello? Who is this?"

But again, no one was there.

It was nearing 1 A.M., Jack Daniels time. I chose to work soberly before then, with the possible exception of a beer before dinner. The discipline of my vices was extremely important to me; but the time was so lonely and the work so intense, that the number of Jacks and smokes had gradually started to increase. I was well aware of this, introspective as I was, but chose not to do anything about it.

There were no chatty phone calls, no gregarious dinners, no strokes of affection. I had run out for a quick bite to eat and saw friends and lovers gathered together, lost in the abandonment of good times: fun, laughter, tenderness. This was all anathema to me. I had only one intention, one will—and that was to paint: to paint if it killed me. If I had to, I would die painting. I would give my life for it, I realized that night, having pizza at Stromboli's, watching the social world around me through the window.

But now with my whiskey and cigarette, gazing at my day's work, I felt the somber satisfaction known only to people who knew no other satisfaction: that I had created something—and that it was something good.

I inhaled my last drag, swigged down the rest of my drink and returned to work. It seemed as if the whole day was a preparation for the deep work at night, when the demons would come out of their hiding places to be exorcized by the colors of my palate. I could be listening to Brahms, Zeppelin, Wagner—it didn't matter. The work took on a flow of its own and I was immersed in the trance of painting, the trance of colors in their perfect places. And I knew—I knew with my soul—where the colors belonged and how they could make life right.

At 2 A.M. it was time for my second Jack and smoke break. I lit up and...ahhh, it was beginning to look good! It was an incredible feeling to set a challenge for yourself and to live up to that challenge. Like a pass-fail exam, you either exceeded your own limitations or you died. Simple as that, I laughed. Wouldn't it be funny— and scary—if the heads of the three men could swivel around completely, their faces as bald as their heads? Ha, ha, ha: this was getting too nightmarish. I had to keep the form, at least, of the barber school. I was not Magritte, after all.

Back to work: I was starting to have a good time. The painting flowed now. I moved like a dancer and swayed to the rhythms of my bright palate: I could paint anything if I could paint this—and I *was* painting this—I was making love to this—I was like a god making love to my painting! I was lifted higher; I was color itself! Ah, the noble joy of being a god and creating a work of art!

It was 3 A.M. and it was time to stop. What a great night of work! I poured myself one final J.D. and lit my goodnight cigarette, staring at my magical mirrors of consciousness. How funny! That's all they were! And the three bald men—who were they? And even worse, who the hell were the barbers? No one knew who he was anyway. And you really had to peer through a lot of mirrors to find out.

I got into bed feeling oh, so nice—even good to be alone, to be a painter, to have worked hard all day long... all day long....

There he was again looking so beautiful, so friendly, so desirable, so godly! I said, "Mercury, my god, I think I'm ready! I'm ready, Mercury!" And my right arm rose by itself in Mercury's direction. My right arm had a will of its own. It reached far, far into the darkness toward Mercury's throne; it reached toward Mercury's perfect body and hovered there, near his wand. It slowly started to move toward the wand...and the telephone rang.

"Hello? Hello? Who the hell is this?"

But there was no one there; there was no one...there.

FOURTEEN

There was no answer when I dialed 586-7601, the number that Star 69 gave me. The calls had continued for several days but I refused to worry about it—it was Sunday and I was looking forward to the Gnostic Mass. I hadn't spoken to John all weekend but my painting was in great shape and just needed a few finishing touches. Can you believe it? It was almost finished!

I was running out for a pizza before the mass when the telephone rang. Should I answer it and try to scare the person? It couldn't possibly be anyone else. I picked up the phone: "Hello, this is Davis. Your call is being recorded by the police and will be directly linked to you. If you want to stay out of prison, please don't call again." And I hung up.

There. That should do it; we'll see if he dares to call again, if it *is* a he. Just out of curiosity, I dialed Star 69 again. Sure enough, it was still 586-7601. Well, I could try calling—nah, let's forget it. Let's go. The telephone rang. Oh, fuck—let the machine get it—I'm outta here! And I slammed my door and ran down the three flights to Ninth Street.

Not being sure if they started on time, I decided to walk with my pizza slice, running a little later than I usually did. I passed the newsstand on St. Marks and Second and saw stacks of Sunday *Times* waiting to be bought. In just one week, I thought, millions of people would be seeing at least one of my paintings in beautiful, living Technicolor! What a thrill! Come on, Davis: don't be so depressed; your life is about to begin! Little did I know how true that was.

I arrived on Lafayette Street and had time to light up before two. There was a small group of cool-looking people smoking: I wondered if they were going where I was going. I tried to hear what they were saying:

"You should have seen him do the Star Ruby!" said one of them to the other. "He jumbled all the Greek and left out the IO Pans entirely!"

Had to be them. Should I introduce myself? No, I'd wait and retain my anonymity a little longer. I took the elevator up with them. "Who's doing it today?" asked a man with long, black hair.

"Jim and Rose," answered a voluptuous woman, dressed in scarlet. "It should be a good one."

The elevator doors opened onto the fourth floor—and there was James with a crowd of Atlantis Bookshop types. "Hey, Davis, 93. You made it. You remember Sam?"

"Of course. Hi Sam, 93."

"93, Davis," she smiled. "Everybody, this is Davis. It's his first mass!"

"93, Davis," they all said.

"Are you sure you know what you're getting yourself into?" kidded the man with the long, black hair. "Once you enter, there's no turning back."

"That's exactly what I'm hoping for," I said, "I hope to never come back."

And they all laughed. I kind of liked this crowd.

"Davis," said Sam, "I'm collecting today; it's a five dollar donation to cover the cost of the studio—if it's your will to pay it, that is."

"Sure, no problem," I said as I coughed up the bucks.

"You might want to untie your shoelaces," James suggested. "They're almost ready and we have to remove our shoes before we enter the temple."

Suddenly everyone turned. "Oh! They're ready! They're ready!" And everybody filed toward the open door of the studio. I could smell the incense coming out of it. Pat was inside to greet us, wearing a white robe with a golden sash, looking very impressive. I immediately noticed a huge altar with candles and roses and black-and-white-checkered steps leading up to it. The altar was surrounded by a blue, starry canopy and covered with red velvet drapery bearing a large, golden star. There were chairs lined up on two sides and several smaller altars between the two rows of chairs. Mysteriously, I felt very much at home.

Pat gave a short introductory talk and began. "Do what thou wilt shall be the whole of the Law!" he announced with outstretched arms. Everyone answered, "Love is the law, love under will."

Now it won't be easy to describe what followed, for I had never witnessed anything like the incredible ceremony I was about to experience. There were so many facets to it; and each phase put me deeper and deeper into a trance. There was hypnotic music, a priest with red and gold robes, and a priestess whom I recognized as Rozelisa, the psychic from Raoul's! I hoped she wouldn't remember me. It felt like being in ancient Egypt—or ancient Greece—or ancient somewhere—with mysterious chants and exotic prayers to gods and goddesses. We kneeled and held hands high in the air; we stood proudly and recited an anthem. It was all deeply meaningful and splendid, unlike any church or synagogue I had ever attended. And it was very, very sexual, as if sex were a natural thing to be celebrated, which of course it was.

Rozelisa sat naked on the altar while the priest charged the "cakes of light"—the wafers—with his rod. Then he did the same with the wine. The power kept getting stronger; I felt like I could rise up out of my chair. The whole intent, it seemed, was for us to be as magical, as powerful as we could be. Then, one by one, we ascended the steps of the altar to receive our cakes of light and cups of wine. When I ate my cake, I felt like the power of the sun was surging through my body; and when I drank the wine, I felt like an ocean of happiness was filling my soul. As instructed, I crossed my arms over my chest in the sign of resurrection and proclaimed, "There is no part of me that is not of the gods!" And I felt truly transformed, truly myself—but in a new way: as if I had taken the power of the gods into myself.

The climax—or to be more accurate, perhaps—the denoument, when the priest blessed us, was beautiful, stunning; I cried. To think that there were people in the world who worshipped the gods within themselves, who *became* gods themselves, as opposed to the common practice of worshipping some old man upstairs with his book of laws, judgments, sins. There was only one law—and that was to honor your own godhood, your own divinity.

Outside on the street the smokers congregated. Lena, the voluptuous woman, chuckled, "If someone could bottle this high! Hear how quiet the traffic is? It's like doing 'shrooms, man."

I looked up at the blue sky and white clouds and pink buildings—and all the friendly people walking the streets—I had never done 'shrooms, but wow! I felt fucking fantastic! "What do they put in those cakes?" I asked Lena.

"Oh, don't worry, honey—no drugs; just a hefty dose of magic. The real thing!"

"Ain't nothin' like the real thing, baby," said Tony, the man with the long, black hair.

"So when's the next one?" I asked.

"The next public one is in July," replied Lena. "But if it's your will to take initiation, then you can come to them all."

"Well," I said, "I'll certainly think about that and discuss it with James. Where *is* James?"

"He must be upstairs, helping them clean up. We smokers get a little break from that."

"Well, it's good to meet you all; I'll probably see you next month."

"93, Davis," they all said.

"93." And I was off to the East Village to finish my painting with an entirely new outlook on life.

Or so I thought. Like most highs, it didn't last forever. And when I returned to eight hang-ups on my machine with no real message, it was pretty tempting to sink into depression again. Should I call John and find out how his party was? Better not, I thought, better get straight to work.

There wasn't that much more to do; if I really concentrated I could finish it by that night. Then I could be free to get in the groove of my upcoming show; I still had all those invitations to mail.

I fixed a cup of tea and put on some Philip Glass: *Einstein on the Beach* seemed like the best inspiration for perfecting *Atlas Barber School*. I studied my work with my tea and cigarette, surveying every inch of the canvas with my fine-tooth-comb of vision. It really was gorgeous but I wanted it sharper, clearer, more pinpointed. If the viewer failed to gasp upon first seeing it, then something was wrong. Just as every word of Crowley's Gnostic Mass seemed perfect, every infinitesimal brushstroke had to be just right.

The phone rang. "Hi. This is Davis. I'm either painting or sleeping. Please leave a message after the tone."

"Hi Davis, it's John. Just calling to see how the painting's going. The party was a success, but we missed having you there. I made my *Crêpes Suzette* and they were a big hit. Call me later if you want. Bye."

Well, what a surprise! John was the last person I expected to hear from—no, actually, Angel was. But I was afraid that if I got engaged in conversation, I would lose my concentration for the painting. So I decided to call him after it was finished. Or maybe I wouldn't call him at all and just send an invitation. I'd see: I would simply "do my will" when the time arrived.

But now my will was to complete my masterpiece; and with its completion, gain the confidence to appear at my show in ten days.

It was done. *Finito.* And it was only 2 A.M. I poured myself a drink and lit a smoke. There it was: perfection. Of course, I'd probably fiddle with it for the next few days, but for the most part, I was satisfied—and I wasn't easily satisfied. Ah, I felt so good! What a great day it had been! Should I go out and celebrate? It was "Sperm" night at The Cock: should I go and mess around?

The phone rang. Nobody called me at 2 A.M. I picked up the receiver and hung it up again. That'd show him! In fact, I went to the wall and unplugged the jack altogether. I did *not* want to be disturbed again. I thought I'd stay home and stare at my painting: nothing could be more of a turn-on. I was actually getting a little sleepy. Why not turn in early? Then I could start my invitations in the morning.

So I gave *Atlas Barber School* one final gaze and got into bed. I tossed and turned for a while, thinking about the Gnostic Mass and how good it felt being there. I thought about Rozelisa's loving smile as she handed me my cake of light. She couldn't have remembered me; she seemed like she was in quite a trance herself. I thought about the taste of the cake and how the wine felt going down. I relived the mass as if I were watching it through a mirror, then two mirrors, then three. I could hear the music of Philip Glass playing. The mass faded and the mirrors became one. I was looking at myself and I was bald. There was a barber behind me and *he* was bald. There was a barber behind him and...I heard laughing. Such sweet laughing! Where was it coming from?

"Here, Davis. I'm right here."

"Mercury, my god! You know I'm ready! I unplugged the phone tonight!"

"I know, Davis; I arranged it all. I always do. Now listen to the music and do your will."

The music repeated and repeated, reverberated and reverberated. I was drawn by the pull of the music, the pull of the darkness, the pull of Mercury's magnetism. My right arm led me as I flew slowly toward Mercury's throne. He smiled as he watched me floating toward him, floating with desire, floating with rapture. My hand was very close to his masculine chest—I could smell his sweet, sensual fragrance—and I lingered there with a longing for the god I wanted so passionately. But my arm was stronger and it drew my hand away; it floated toward the wand…closer, closer, closer—and my hand reached out and grasped the wand.

Suddenly the music changed and the sky opened and everything turned lavender. The music sounded like angels singing and lavender light glimmered over the wand. It vibrated in my hand and glowed bright white. And it started to transform before my eyes: it became a conductor's baton, then a writer's quill, and finally a painter's brush. It changed colors continuously, each one more beautiful than the next.

We were traveling somewhere, Mercury and I together; we were traveling upward, upward into the lavender light. We were together; we were companions, but others were traveling with us, further away. Where were we going? Where were we flying? The music kept getting higher and it felt like we were ascending to an altitude of ecstatic heights.

And we were there. I held the wand tightly and Mercury looked very proud. All the gods and goddesses surrounded us. There was an enormous throne with a king sitting on it—and suddenly I knew where we were.

I started to cry with the realization: we were in Olympus.

"Welcome to Olympus, Lord Davis, and congratulations on your noble choice. I am Jupiter, also known as Zeus, king of the gods. You have not chosen to paint me, but I understand the reason why: you did not know me before. For 34 years you have walked the surface of the earth for the purpose of reaching this night. You chose the more difficult choice. Most people would choose Mercury here, looking so beautiful and young, smiling his charming smile; most people want love and happiness in their lives—and pray to a god, hoping to have it. But you did not choose love; you did not choose happiness. You chose the caduceus wand of magical power—you have chosen to be one of us, one of the creators. As you have seen, the wand can take any form. Use it well, Lord Davis, as the artist you are, and always remember your divinity."

I wanted to thank Jupiter but everything vanished at that moment and I was transported back through the lavender light, back through space, back to earth…and I drifted into a deep sleep, forgetting on a conscious level all that had occurred, ready to live my life as the god I had become.

FIFTEEN

I had become quite prolific in the days before my show; it seemed like I was burning to churn out my "Absurdity of Life" series. In one week I had completed another major work, *Eating at Stromboli's: A Solitary Slice,* and was very pleased with it. The painting showed me from behind, sitting alone in the large window, eating my slice as I watched the world go by. Friends and lovers paraded before me, oblivious to their observer. And now, the day of my opening, I was pretty far along with *Self-Portrait as Parsifal*, the work I had envisioned for some time. The dying swan with its tragic beauty was perfect—but how would the viewer know that I was receiving the Grail for the last time? The answer had to lie in the expression of my eyes—and that was the challenge that still plagued me.

I was feeling more self-assured, perhaps, than I'd ever felt in my life and was finally ready for the big night. My parents had flown in from Florida, my sister and brother-in-law from Chicago. John responded to his invitation and said he'd definitely be there, even though we hadn't seen each other since the night of our candlelit dinner. And there was no response from Angel.

The Sunday *Times* article looked great—they had printed only *Mercury and Diana,* which was fine with me—and I got calls from people all over the country. Speaking of calls, the anonymous ones gradually tapered off; but John and I were barely talking to each other. I was just too busy to see him, which he found difficult to understand.

I was meeting my family for a drink at the Empire Diner on 10th Avenue before the reception. It was an early summer evening at the end of June and I felt surprisingly calm. I arrived first and chose an outside table. I wore pretty much my standard uniform: black boots, black jeans, and the nice black shirt I had bought in London several trips before.

A taxi pulled up and my family got out. It was good to see them: I gave my mother a big hug and kissed the other three. They were all dressed up, as usual, the men wearing jackets and ties.

We had a pleasant visit after the preliminary congratulations were out of the way, my father and brother-in-law discussing their respective businesses and my mother and sister discussing their day's adventure at Saks. I was eager to get to the gallery, so I suggested that we walk over to 24th Street. It was getting exciting! And all I had to do was be charming and social, two of my most natural talents.

As we strolled over to 24th Street, a little more slowly than I would have liked, I walked next to my mother. "Why did you get your hair cut so short, Davey?" she asked.

"Oh, I don't know, Mom, I just felt like it, I guess. Yours looks nice," I said, trying to change the subject, "and you've got such a nice tan."

"Your father and I are so pleased for you, honey. It looks like your time has finally arrived."

"Thanks, Mom. Yeah, I'm feeling good about it. I'm looking forward to introducing you to Jessica from London. She's so wonderful and she's the one who's responsible for all of this."

"You really should get her something nice. Did you do that?"

"Not yet. But I'd like to take her out for dinner when we've all calmed down a bit. Oh God—we're almost there!" I shouted to everyone. "See down there? It's the last gallery on the right!"

It looked like people were starting to arrive; there was

a long, black limousine right out front. I suddenly felt like I was going to throw up.

"Are you OK, Davis?" my sister asked.

"Oh yeah, I'm fine—I just might be violently ill and have to go home! Just kidding; I'm really all right."

And with my family I passed through the grand doors of Gagosian Gallery, having arrived at last, with the first people I ever knew, onto the big scene of the New York Art World.

The difference between a snob and an elitist is this: a snob refuses to have instant coffee; while an elitist insists on having the *best* coffee, whether it's instant or not. And there were several instant coffees I used to know that were excellent, as long as you made them strong enough.

The point I'm making is this: it's amazing how people will listen to whatever you have to say when you're "somebody"—but would ignore the identical words if you were "nobody." I was used to being a "nobody" most of my life; but when I walked through the doors of Gagosian Gallery with my proud family, I could have uttered the most inane witticisms—and they would have been perfectly acceptable. People are such snobs. I should know: I was such an elitist!

The first person I saw was Julia from *The New York Times*. "Davis! Look at your paintings over there! How do you feel on the night of your big opening?"

"Uh, I don't know, Julia. Am I being interviewed? I feel really strange, I guess."

And everyone in the vicinity roared with laughter. See what I mean? I could have said anything. "Julia, the article was good. These are my parents—Mom and Dad, this is Julia who wrote the Sunday article. And this is my sister Evelyn and her husband Bruce."

"So nice to meet you all; you've got such a talented son—and brother!"

"Oh, we've always known that," said my father, "ever since we got him his first set of paints when he was three." (In reality, my father thought I spent too much time at my easel and wanted to encourage more manly activities like building blocks and trucks.)

"Hello, hello!" crooned Jessica, appearing on the scene. We gave each other a big hug and kiss.

"Jessica—it's so good to see you."

"Let me get you some champagne, darling, I'll be right back."

Flash! There was Chris, taking a picture of me. "Hi Chris! How ya doin' man?" I still didn't know what *his* scene was. Maybe I'd find out by the end of the evening.

"Davis, the star! I pushed for both pictures, but they just wanted one for each artist."

"Oh, that's OK: it looked super."

And before Jessica returned, a handsome waiter arrived to serve champagne to all of us. "Here's to my soon-to-be-rich brother-in-law!" toasted Bruce.

"Hear, hear," everyone answered.

"Oh Davis, I see you have your champagne. Well, take another—you're going to need it."

"Thanks, Jessica, you are a lifesaver in every conceivable way. Mom and Dad, this is Jessica, my angel from heaven."

"Delighted to meet you. You've got a very special son."

"That's what we tried to tell him," joked my mother, "but it took a long time for him to believe it. Jessica, we've heard so much about you. It's so wonderful what you've done for Davis."

"Oh posh, he did it all himself. He works so hard. Come, have you seen the paintings yet? Let's have a family viewing."

Uh-oh. Here was the moment I was dreading: all the gods and goddesses, especially the men, were graphically nude. What would they say? We all walked over to my area on the west side of the gallery. My four creations were arranged and hung with expert, professional care: they looked terrific, I must say. Everyone was silent. Finally my sister said, "They're really gorgeous, Davis."

"Thank you, Evelyn; that means a lot to me."

"They're so *artistic*!" exclaimed my mother.

"Very impressive," said my father, looking right at Diana's Ultramarine Violet nipples.

"Davis," Bruce said, "I've got to hand it to you. I think you've got a gold mine here, a virtual gold mine."

"Let's hope so!" I laughed as I swigged down my second champagne.

"Davis, darling, there's someone I want you to meet," said Jessica. "This is Jeremy. He's known your work for quite some time."

"How are you, Jeremy? Good to meet you."

"A pleasure, Davis. They're beautiful, just beautiful."

"Thank you."

It's funny when your head knows just when to turn: there was John entering the gallery with Ludwig. Oh great. What should I do? "Excuse me a minute, folks, I want to say hello to someone." I decided to go right up to them and get it over with.

"Hi John, Ludwig. I'm glad you both could come."

"Davis, good to see you, buddy," said John, shaking my hand in that firm, serious way of his.

"This is so thrilling, Davis!" exclaimed Ludwig. "Are you having a good time?"

"I think so," I said. "I can't quite believe that it's happening. John, would you like to have a cigarette outside? I could use one."

"I've quit actually, but I'll go with you, if you like. Ludwig, would you excuse us for a minute?"

Ludwig looked a little taken aback as we passed through the substantial crowd that was now forming; I hoped we'd be able to make it to the door without being accosted. "Hey Davis, 93!" There was James with his wife, Christina.

"James, 93. This is John; John this is Christina. Listen, you guys, we're trying to get out for a smoke. We'll see you in a bit."

We finally cleared the doors and walked out onto a sunset to die for over the Hudson. "Hi John. It's good to see you. It means a lot to me that you came."

"Are you kidding, Davis? I wouldn't have missed this…"

"Let's take a little walk and look at the sunset."

"Sunsets are always exciting with you," he said, "just like your paintings."

"Oh, you always know the right things to say—when you decide to say them," I teased.

"Well, I've decided that this is the right time," he winked.

We smiled at each other, just like the old days, and we walked silently for a while. It was good to take a break from the festivities but I didn't know what more to say. He reached out to hold my hand but I couldn't cling to him for too long. "I should be getting back, I suppose," I said.

"Yeah, Davis, it is your party, after all."

And we walked back together.

Another snob story: once I was at a luncheon with other art students and they served delicious French food on paper plates with plastic knives and forks. I couldn't believe that so many people were complaining about the food. Believe me, it was truly *la crème de la crème.* That very same night—and I kid you not—I happened to be dining in a pretty French restaurant on Theater Row. The food was awful, but it was served on elegant china, arranged artfully on the plate. No one knew the difference except me: I sent my *saumon à la moutarde* back. You see? In general, people just don't know; but they *think* they do in a big way. So if paintings are hanging in an impressive gallery, they've got to be good, right?

We walked through the doors and who should be there to shake my hand but the world-renowned sculptor, Jay Zaso, whose pieces were also in the show. He had just been commissioned to do a major installation at the Guggenheim Bilbao in Spain.

"Davis," he said.

"Jay," I said, "It's such an honor to be in the same show with you. This really is a step up for me."

"Davis, the honor is mine. Your pieces are lovely. This is my wife, Betty."

"Hello, Betty, nice to meet you."

"The same, Davis. Where did you get the idea to paint all those gods and goddesses? And in such an original way!"

"I don't know. It all came to me in a dream. Oh, John, I'm sorry. This is John Cunningham. John, Jay and Betty Zaso." I was doing the best I could. Out of the corner of my eye, I couldn't believe what I saw: Ludwig was eating *hors d'oeuvres* with Chris and seemed to be flirting with him.

Suddenly Jessica appeared. "Davis, darling, I want you to meet Edward Pearson from the Metropolitan Museum." Then she whispered in my ear, "He's been eyeing *Mercury and Diana* for a very long time. I think he wants to buy it!"

"Mr. Pearson," I said, "So nice to meet you. What do you think of the show?" I couldn't think of anything else to say.

"I'm enthralled, Davis. Tell me, how long did it take for you to complete *Mercury and Diana on the Way to Olympus?*"

"Oh, let me see…I think it was about three hours—

no, just kidding—about three months. Usually it takes me a week or so—but that's when I don't eat or sleep!"

"Ha, ha," Mr. Pearson laughed. "I bet you'll get a good sleep after *this* is over!"

"I don't know; I'm in the middle of a problematic self-portrait. I should go study my face in the men's room."

And everybody laughed, of course. Where was a waiter with some champagne? Instead of becoming more relaxed, it seemed like I was becoming more and more nervous. Where was the backbite of the art world, the familiar sense of cynicism? Somehow, that would have been easier to handle. "Will you all excuse me a moment? Women can say they're going to powder their noses; I'll just stick with the studying-my-face excuse."

And again they all laughed, like characters in a nightmare.

I walked straight to the nearest handsome waiter, grabbed a glass of champagne and tried to get to the men's room without being stopped. *En route*, I noticed Ludwig, still flirting with Chris. I surreptitiously walked near them and saw Ludwig writing something on one of the invitations. Without being noticed, I tried to sneak behind them to see what was going on. This wasn't easy to do at a party where everyone knew who I was, but I was determined to pull it off. It looked like Ludwig was writing down his telephone number. I nearly dropped my champagne glass and thought I was going to pass out: the number that Ludwig gave Chris was 586-7601.

The guard let me through and I was glad that there were four private bathrooms; I locked myself in one of them and felt like staying there forever. Ludwig was the anonymous caller! (Of course, how obvious!) I would just confront him with it—that's what I was going to do. I didn't pass out; instead, I splashed some cold water on my face and reentered the gallery proper to confront

101

Ludwig. Ah, another champagne—just what I needed! They were small, anyway.

But before I could find Ludwig, there was Aaron, one of the dealers who had come to my studio. "Aaron, it is such a thrill to be a part of this show."

"Davis, it's a pleasure to have you in it. Everyone loves your work. And there's a good chance that the Met will buy one."

"That's what Jessica told me. Not to jinx it, but how good do you think the chances are?"

"In this business, you never know. All we know is that your work is good and deserves to be sold."

"Thank you, Aaron, that's the best compliment I could receive. Oh, here's my mother. Hi Mom, this is Aaron, one of the art dealers who chose my paintings."

"Nice to meet you, Aaron, I think you made a very good choice. But I'm prejudiced, of course!"

"You have every right to be; he's a gifted painter. Excuse me. Nice to see you both."

"How are you, Mom? Are you having a good time?"

"Oh, just wonderful, Davey, but I'm looking for the ladies' room."

"Well, tell the guard over there that you're my mother and he'll let you in. Only exclusive people get to use the facilities here. See you later." And I resumed my hunt for Ludwig.

Instead I encountered John, inspecting Jay Zaso's work. "How do you like it?" I asked him.

"Not too much, Davis; I much prefer yours."

"Thank you, John, but mine is easy to like. This stuff is truly great: look how that arm reaches up into infinity."

"Yeah, but I'd like to see more than just the arm."

"That's the whole point; there *is* nothing more than the arm, nothing more than the reaching. Anyway, I'm looking for Ludwig. Have you seen him?"

"He's over there, flirting with that cute photographer."

"Oh, still? Will you excuse me, sir? There's something I need to ask him."

"It's your party."

And I sauntered over to Chris and Ludwig in their new location, engaged in laughter. "Chris, hi. I see you've become acquainted with Ludwig. Ludwig, may I talk to you for a second? There's something I need to ask you."

"What is it about, Davis?"

"It's kind of private. You'll know in a minute. Excuse us, Chris—this won't take long."

"Sure, Davis."

"What is the problem, Davis?"

"Ludwig, have you been calling me?"

"What do you mean? I called you once to inform you of John's cat."

"Let's get real, Ludwig. I know it's been you. Why have you been calling me?"

"Davis, I…"

"*Why have you been calling me?*"

He paused. "Do you really want to know the answer?"

"Of course I do; that's why I'm asking."

"I'm not sure this is the best time to tell you."

"Look, just tell me and then get out of here."

"All right. The reason I've been calling you is to find out if you have been home."

"What?"

"I have needed to know if you have been home or not."

"And why should you need to know that?"

"So that I could be with John, of course, what do you think? That weekend when John's cat was sick—remember? You didn't return his call. He was very upset that Sunday night after a grueling weekend. He needed comfort and I was there to give it to him. I've been giving it to him ever since. It's good that you are out of the picture now. You could never give him what he needs."

I was totally silent and didn't know what to say. Finally, feeling like I might cry, I asked, "How can you tell me this during my show, Ludwig?"

"You asked for it, Davis."

"Would you please get out of here now?"

"Keep your voice down. People are turning around."

"Let them turn around and bring the police with them. Get the fuck out of my show please."

"What seems to be the problem, Davis?" asked John, arriving on the scene.

"I've asked Ludwig to leave and I'd appreciate it if you'd leave with him. You deserve each other."

"What are you talking about?"

"All that time you lied to me, John."

"Davis…"

"It's funny: I don't know why I always imagine that people will be honest with me." And I walked out the front door as everyone turned and wondered what was happening.

When depression hits, it hits very hard, like a mild toothache that suddenly reaches the nerve. I paced around the block, smoking, deciding what to do. I couldn't go back in there and face all those people. But I had to; my family was there and we were going out to dinner. How could I possibly continue the evening? How could I possibly say another charming word? There was only one solution: I would tell them I wasn't feeling well, that I had to go home. What a disaster! But I had to do it. "Do what thou wilt shall be the whole of the Law." I had to return to my painting. It was the only thing that mattered. I knew the expression for the eyes now. I neared the doors of the gallery with firm resolve. I would tell my parents I was taking a taxi. I had to start painting immediately. So I opened the doors of Gagosian Gallery; and I saw in their reflection the hopelessness in my eyes.

SIXTEEN

My eyes were perfected and the painting was finished. It was the most honest piece of work I'd ever done. I hadn't slept for two nights but I wasn't tired. I had been drinking pretty heavily and smoking non-stop. In a way I was totally zonked; yet I felt very light, as if I weren't in full possession of my mind. The process had been excruciating, seeing my own sorrow magnified and mirrored back at me. But it was finally finished and I was free.

I got out a beer and sat down to listen to my phone messages. My hands were shaking slightly. I hadn't answered the phone since the day of my opening; I had turned off the ringer and the volume. So early in the evening I decided to listen to two days worth of calls. This is what I heard:

"Davey—it's Mom. Just calling to see if you're OK. We've all been worried about you. This is our last day in the city and we hope to see you. So please call us at the hotel, OK? We love you."

"Hey, it's James. 93—Thursday at 12:30. Too bad we didn't get to spend any time with you last night. But your paintings were very cool. Talk to you later. 93."

"Hello, this is Shirley Foster and I'm calling from New Haven. I'd like to talk about commissioning you to paint some gods and goddesses for our living room. Please call me at 203-758-4982. Thank you."

"Davis, it's Jessica here. Are you all right? Last night was a big success. Have you heard from the gallery yet? The Met is going to buy your painting! Call me soon, darling."

"Davis, this is Aaron at Gagosian. Good news! You've broken six figures! Ed Pearson wants to buy *Mercury and*

Diana. Please call me right away. Thanks."

"Davis, this is Dad. We're wondering where you are. It's getting close to dinner time and we haven't heard from you. We're very proud of you and would love to see you before we leave tomorrow. Please call us. What? Mom says to tell you we'll be at La Goulue Restaurant at 7:30. Hope to see you there."

"Hi Davis, it's John. I don't suppose you want to hear from me, but there are a few things I'd like to say. First, it's true that Ludwig was always just my friend—at least when I told you he was. I never really lied to you, but later couldn't bring myself to tell you the whole truth. You were always my number one choice and maybe it's time to say what I never did before: I love you, Davis. Please call me."

Then there were three hang-ups in a row. I didn't think they were from Ludwig.

"Hi Davis, it's Evelyn. It's Friday morning and we're at the airport. We're all worried sick about you, Davey. Are you all right? Please call us all at home and let us know if you're OK. Love you."

"Mr. Jarvey, this is Ned Levy calling from Las Vegas. Please call me at your earliest convenience. I'd like to hire you to do the artwork for our new casino/resort. You can reach me at 702-489-9390. Looking forward to talking with you."

"Davis! Have you seen the *Times* today? This is Jessica. It's glowing: he calls *Mercury and Diana* 'breathtaking.' And listen to this: 'An artist with a vast scope of vision, a sense of integrity that is rare in this day and age.' Congratulations, darling—call me!"

"Hello, Davis. This is Sue at Gagosian Gallery. Please call us; Aaron wants to talk to you. Thanks a lot, Davis."

"Davis, this is Stephen calling from London. I saw the *Times* review on the Internet. Congratulations—it's wonderful! Call me and tell me all about the opening. I can't wait to hear! Bye, Davis."

"Hi Davis, it's John. I'd really like to talk to you. I'll be working late in the office tonight so you can reach me here. Please call me, Davis."

And I stopped the machine. I finished my beer, brushed my teeth and washed my face. I got dressed and ready for the 6 Train. I was going to John's office to confront him in person.

I tried to act as normal as possible when signing in with the guard downstairs. I told him I was going to Intelligentsia and that I was expected. I was alone in the elevator and, like a Bowery bum, pulled out my little bottle of Jack Daniels and took a swig. I had to keep the edge off; for without any sleep, everything seemed to be getting edgier and edgier.

The elevator opened onto the 44th floor. I tried to see if I could walk a straight line to John's office. "The shortest distance between two points is a straight line, Davis," I said to myself, knowing that I failed the test. I buzzed the buzzer. I waited. There didn't seem to be an answer. I buzzed the buzzer again. Could he have gone already? I buzzed three long buzzes.

"Coming, coming," I heard. The door opened and we were face to face.

"Surprise," I announced.

"Davis—I can't believe it. Come in."

"What took you so long to get to the door? I thought you weren't there."

"I was working in my private office. There's an auction on Monday and I have to do some research for it."

"Oh: research. I get it."

"Davis, you're drunk."

"Drunk? No; I just haven't slept in three days. I finished my self-portrait. It's the best thing I've ever done."

"That's saying a lot, after the *Times* review today. Did

you see it?"

"No. I haven't seen anything. So: John. Are you alone here? Is Ludwig naked in your office or something?"

"Don't be silly, I'm quite alone—and *feeling* quite alone. You got my messages, I take it?"

"Oh yeah, when you told me you loved me? Well, guess what, John? I loved you too. But I love my work more!"

"I'm beginning to come around to that realization. Why don't you come in and sit down?"

"What if I don't want to sit down?"

"Well, fine, we'll just stand here, then. Why don't I make you some coffee?"

"No thanks, lover man, but would you like some J.D.?" I took out my bottle and offered him a drink.

"Thank you, I'm working. Why don't you put that away? I think you've had enough."

"Enough? Yeah, you're damn right I've had enough. Enough of dishonest, cowardly people in this world." And I took a big drink. "Are you a man of your word or are you a liar? There's no in-between."

"Davis, it's not going to be easy to talk to you like this. How can I get you to forgive me?"

"Forgive you? You know, John, what does it matter if someone fucks around a little? That's not my gripe: it's only natural. I don't care who you fuck around with; no one has the right to demand control of another person's body. Monogamy is the biggest lie of all. I don't care two fucks for monogamy. What I care two fucks for is a little trust, which I thought we had. All that time, all those weeks, you were messing around with that contemptible, sniveling phony. Just because he's a blond hunk—just so you could have some 'comfort' during the week until you saw me on the weekend. It's your deceitful behavior that I have contempt for—you and everyone else in this 'world of men' who don't know how to stand up and *be* men."

"Davis, I'm not sure if we should continue this conversation."

"Why not? You're the one who wanted to have it."

"I'm not sure that you're in any condition…"

"Condition? What kind of condition? I'm in the best condition I could possibly be in! Vulnerable and strung out on reality! Raw and passionate with the truth! What better condition is there?"

"Why don't we talk tomorrow? I think you should go home now."

"Oh, you are just too much. First you beg me to call you and then you ask me to leave! What do you want, Mr. Autograph Dealer? Do you want me to write you a letter that you could sell for a million dollars?"

"Davis…"

"Don't 'Davis' me—and don't raise your hand up at me when I'm trying to talk to you!" I took his hand and twisted it around; but he gained control and pushed my body back.

"Davis, you better get out of here. You're out of control."

"*I'm* out of control? What about you? I'm the one *in* control!" And I forced myself on him: I pushed him up against the Ibsen case.

"Please be careful. This is glass!"

"Oh, yes. We better be careful. We better not damage the goods! Well, *I* feel damaged! I feel cheated! It doesn't matter that our relationship has been dwindling away; what matters is human decency, the human respect of one man for another!" And I raised my right arm in defiance of the world's corruption, and I flung it in John's direction. It hit him in his face.

"Fuck you, Davis, you're going to get violent with me?"

"Maybe physical violence is better than the emotional

violence we all inflict on each other."

"Oh, you are so brilliant; you're such a fucking genius!"

And I hurled my fist at his head—but he ducked and I smashed the glass of the Ibsen case. A loud alarm went off. My blood spattered the Ibsen letter.

"Oh my God, Davis!"

I felt like I was in another world. The alarm was like a siren inside my mind, urging me to do what I had to do. There were two available pistols. I reached in and grabbed one of them. It felt good in my hand.

"Put that down! It might be loaded!"

"Oh, really now! Why don't we just test it out?" I cocked the pistol like a gunslinger in a western film; and aiming for Meri's desk, I pulled the trigger. BOOM! Her vase of roses shattered all over the floor, the gun smoking in my hand.

"DAVIS!" screamed John, "Put that down! The police will be here any minute! Put that gun down!"

"John. I've never seen you so hysterical. And with good reason! What power I have in my bleeding hand! Here's to all the liars in the gay world!" And I fired a shot at the ceiling. "And here's to all the liars in the straight world!" And I fired a shot at the door. "And here's to…" And I aimed the gun at John.

"Davis. Put that gun down. Please. This has really gotten out of hand. Put the gun down, Davis."

"Why should I do that?"

"Because I'm somebody who loves you."

"You love me? What a laugh! I've had it with that sentimental crap: it doesn't exist. It's a Hollywood fantasy. The only thing that exists is you and me and this gun—life and death."

"*Please*, Davis…"

"I'm going to put an end to it, John. And by putting an end to it I will avenge the lies of this world."

Then everything happened all at once. The alarm

seemed to get much louder, throbbing inside my head—there was a pounding at the door—and John started to cry, dropping down to the floor. I saw the anguished look in his eyes and I saw my bleeding hand holding the gun—and I realized I could never kill him. I could never kill another person.

The pounding at the door continued. "Open up! Security!"

Surrounded by a world of lies and deceit, where love was next to impossible, I realized that the only person I could ever kill was myself. Why should I stay in this world any longer? I had to get away from it.

"Security! Open up!"

I cocked the pistol and held it to my head.

"DAVIS! NO!"

Do it beautifully, Eilert Løvborg, with vine leaves in your hair. I pulled the trigger. And it shot off like an orgasm into my mind.

SEVENTEEN

My mind felt very peaceful. But my head lay splattered on the floor. Blood was everywhere. It was a little confusing; how could I be watching all of this? My body was sprawled out on the floor, the pistol beside it. John was sobbing hysterically over my body—but I couldn't hear anything. I seemed to be floating over all of this, looking down. The security guard and two policemen entered the scene. They looked like they were trying to talk to John, but he kept sobbing and sobbing.

I didn't quite know what to do. Nothing made sense but I felt so free of any kind of pain: just very, very peaceful. It seemed like I had three choices. I could enter this dark, scary-looking tunnel that was down near my body; or I could linger in John's office and watch what was going on; or I could travel upwards into this shimmering passageway of white light. The first two choices seemed very unpleasant to me; so I chose the third choice and entered into the white light.

Whoosh! I was propelled upward, like Alice falling down the rabbit hole, only in reverse. I could see John's office fading away, getting smaller and smaller, until it didn't exist any longer. I traveled for a long time through this beautiful white light and it felt so good. I didn't understand what was happening but I was enjoying the experience. There was crystal-like dust all around me and very strange music playing, almost like the ambient sounds at Charles de Gaulle Airport in Paris. A cool wind seemed to be breezing over my body—but where *was* my body? I couldn't see it—and it felt like I was having a flying dream, only it was real. It reminded me of the one time in my life when I parachuted, after the chute had opened, when I floated with a still, quiet calm.

It seemed like I was nearing the end of the tunnel. It was so pleasant that I was sorry the trip was almost over. Where was I going? What was happening? The answers didn't seem important; it just felt so peaceful.

At the top of the tunnel were my grandparents—I couldn't believe it—and the Siamese cat that I had as a child! They were all welcoming me and it felt so good. They didn't actually talk; but they seemed to project their thoughts into my mind. They explained that I had passed over to the other side and that they would be escorting me to the gates of my temporary home. What was my new home going to be? They seemed to read my thought and replied that it was like a school—an extraordinary school—and that everyone went there after crossing over.

What kind of school, I wondered. A school to understand the meaning of life, they answered. How happy I felt! So there was a meaning to life after all? Oh yes, they smiled, and I would soon be remembering it, for I had learned it all before. My class, they projected, was a very unusual one, and some of my favorite people had gone to it, Kurt Cobain and Sarah Kane, to name but a few. What kind of class was this, I wondered. A class for geniuses who ended their own lives, as geniuses were often tempted to do. Does this mean that I was a genius, then? Yes, they replied, but all genius means is attaining a higher creative state than most people are able to attain—a higher vibration, yet a difficult one to maintain on the earth plane. But you will learn all of this in the class, they explained.

I didn't feel nervous or apprehensive at all. Everything felt just right, just like it was supposed to be. And it was so good to see my grandparents and cat again. Wait a minute—it was my mother's Siamese cat who died and *also* my childhood cat that I had later. They were one in the same cat! That's right, they vibrated, animals come back to be with their families. This was all just lovely. There was no pain, no worry; just a serene feeling of perfection, the kind of perfection I had always desired.

My grandparents, cat and I floated for a while through a blue mist. Everything I'm describing to you now is not exactly as it was—for there are no words to describe what it really was like there. The blue mist was so beautiful, like the foggiest day you can imagine, only bright blue.

Finally we arrived at these silver gates, which opened all by themselves. And my grandparents and cat seemed to bid me good-bye, with the promise of meeting me again soon. The keeper of the gate brought me to my dwelling place, a translucent bubble of light, almost like the bubble in Bosch's *Garden of Delights*, where I would await my first class.

There didn't seem to be any need for eating or sleeping, so I entered the bubble and felt suddenly energized, while still very peaceful. The only feeling I could compare it to was a hit of pure cocaine. I got the impression that I could choose any shape or age I wanted; so I chose myself at age 27 and saw a form of myself appear. I would find out later that Shaw was quite right in his play, *Man and Superman*: after death, you could appear as any age you liked. And to me 27 was the perfect age.

I heard a bell chiming, signaling the first class. The bubble disappeared and I was flying with other— what?—souls?—to the class. It all seemed perfectly natural; and I felt I had gone through this experience many times before. We entered what looked like a crystal palace and there was our Master Teacher, welcoming us back. I felt a special kinship with the other souls in the class; there were about twenty of us. And Eurasma, the name of our Master Teacher, was the purest, most radiant being I had ever encountered.

He explained that there would be eleven classes. Each

class would instruct us on the purpose and meaning of life. But *our* class was so unique, that after the last one was finished, we would all have the privilege of being propelled straight back to earth to do it all over again! All of us groaned.

We were given an assignment that was due by the eleventh class: to write a book about our suicides. As an incentive, I suppose, Eurasma told us that one of our books would be chosen for publication on the earth plane. He revealed that he had a material connection with a publisher in New Orleans and that he promised him the best manuscript from the class. So all of us were to work very hard on the story of our suicides—and one of them would be selected.

There was just a brief lesson in the first class. We were told that the purpose of life was for the soul to learn. Through difficult and negative experiences, the soul would grow and gradually become purified. Then the class was over and we all flew back to our bubbles to begin writing our end-of-life stories.

I've always known, ever since I was a little boy, that one day I would kill someone…. Life is full of surprises, but death is full of certainty…. It hits you like a bell that chimes, urging you to return to your seat, warning you that the drug of slowly-played music, the narcotic of soothing, calm existence, awaits. The bell chimes. You can hear it on the balcony, the smoke-filled balcony under the nearly-full moon, with the space and the air and the interval between the acts: the breathing-space that we all need to survive… until we encounter the next act, the next context, the next chapter….

So here I am in my bubble of light, finishing my story before the last class. We have learned many things here, most of them simple—all of them sublime. I'm not going to tell you all I've learned: you'll be reminded soon enough. What I *will* tell you, though, is that life tests you constantly—and you either rise or fall with each new test. Everything: the good, the bad, the horrendous—is all about the growth of the soul. Each life we have teaches us something; but suicide thwarts the very teaching we were meant to have.

Does God exist? Well, that's a big question! Let me answer it simply by saying that all Gods are one—and they are all to be found within you.

Ah, I hear the bell chiming and I have to finish up. I hope my manuscript is selected because I would like my story to help others who might need to hear it. Remember what Ouspensky said? "In order to help others one must first learn to be an egoist, a conscious egoist. Only a conscious egoist can help people." I would be happy if I knew my life had that purpose.

Most people, after completing their classes, go to a place of consciousness that is commonly known as heaven—and it's supposed to be even more blissful than where we are now. They get to spend a long time there before returning to earth for their next life. We suicides have to go right back, though. Now life may be cruel, but death certainly isn't; and we've been told we're going to get a glimpse of heaven before we return. Plus I've learned that any concept of God we had on earth will be there to greet us. I do look forward to seeing Mercury again. After all, I've got his caduceus wand.

Well, the bell has chimed once more and the bubble is vanishing as I finish writing. Soon I'll be getting a glimpse of heaven! And then it's back to earth for the next life. There I'll be seeing John and Angel and Jessica and Ludwig and James and Stephen and my mother, my father and my sister. And *this* time…I'm really going to try to get it right.

AUTHOR'S NOTE

In "real life" Sarah Kane was my close friend. In many respects, the writing of this book has helped me to deal with the pain of losing her. She never attended an art opening of mine because in "real life" I have never been a painter. I tried to create something that she might have said under the circumstances, something that was very Sarah. And I created Davis's suicide to try to understand hers better. Everyone seems to want a logical explanation for suicide; but in my experience, especially with Sarah, this is often not possible. But you can see and read her plays, now performed all over the world.